OFFED
A Novel

GARY D. RHODES

Published in the USA by:
BearManor Media
1317 Edgewater Drive #110
Orlando, Florida 32804
www.bearmanormedia.com

ISBN 978-1-62933-538-4

Printed in the United States of America.

OFFED

CHAPTER 1

Endings

"I chose because I had no choice."

That had a pretty good sound to it. I wondered if anybody had ever said it before. Maybe. Probably, even, but when you get right down to it, famous quotations aren't usually all that famous.

Anyhow, there I was, on my way to shake hands with the President of the United States. And in style, because he sent for me. Somebody at the White House called my agent, who called my manager, who called yours truly. That meant checking my schedule, but in fairness I would have cancelled any prior engagement. You don't turn down the President. It doesn't matter if you voted for someone else, or if you didn't vote at all. You just don't turn down the President.

As far as getting to the White House, I hated every minute of the journey. The airports and the traffic, and God, how I despise taxis. The cabbies always have to talk to me, or hound me for autographs. Limo drivers are no different. And sure enough, today's guy opened his mouth right quick.

"Sorry about this," he said, using the rear view mirror to stare at me with unblinking intensity. "Looks like we're stuck for a few minutes."

Another red light, dammit. And my new friend was chewing gum, way too loud for his own good.

"No problemo."

I regretted opening my mouth. Even a brief response could signal the start of a conversation, and I didn't even know if this guy actually worked for the White House or if he was just a hired hand. Either way, he kept right on talking, and smacking his Juicy Fruit or Big Red or whatever it was.

"So, it's really you back there, huh?"

"Yup," I agreed in a tone of voice that wasn't very agreeable.

"Birch, am I right?"

"Yup."

"Birch, uhh…?"

"That's me."

"Birch, uhh…uhh…"

"Birch Barr."

"Yeah, Birch Barr, right? Am I right? Huh? Tell me I'm right."

"Dead to rights, pal."

"The kids won't believe this. I drive these politicians around all day, and the occasional movie star, but this, I mean, hey, this is really something, know what I mean?"

After he spit out the last word, he munched his gum for all it was worth.

"That's mighty kind of you," I said, sighing as my words trailed off into the sunset.

"You look a lot shorter in person."

"I'm sitting down."

"Course you are. So look, how does a guy actually get into your line of work?"

His cell phone rang.

"Hold on! I gotta take this," he said to me, right before yapping into the receiver.

In today's world, people are so rude with the phones and the talking and the texting. One thing's for sure: I'm not suited to the twentieth century, and I say that knowing it's the twenty-first.

I grabbed a Brach's butterscotch out of my pocket and unwrapped it. If he was gonna chew, I was damn sure gonna suck.

"Sorry 'bout that," he apologized. "So, you were gonna tell me how you got into your career there."

It began again.

"I chose because I had no choice."

The words fell out of my mouth like a hooked fish onto the deck of an old boat.

"That's really something."

"Well, thanks partner, but if you don't mind…"

I cleared my throat and avoided further eye contact. This joker probably didn't even have a security clearance. I might have sighed again, but I'm not sure. Maybe that one was just in my head. Days like this are exactly why my psychiatrist recommended upping my dosage from 20 to 40 milograms. I had refused that advice, mainly because a guy like me can't afford to get numbed out.

"Of course. You probably have to concentrate on your meeting. You gonna give the President a personal demonstration, huh? I wish you would! You know, I didn't vote for the schmuck myself. He ain't *my* President."

"Yeah, well. I better look over my notes."

In all honesty, my notes amounted to nothing more than some scraps of paper bouncing around inside my otherwise empty briefcase. It was a new case. Nice leather. Smelled good. And black is the new black.

The clasps made a great pop sound when I pushed the two buttons to open it. Sometimes I snapped the clasps back down and opened them up again, just to hear that sound. It wasn't a pop, really. But it wasn't a clink either. More of a quick thunk, or a thunk-thunk if one of my thumbs was faster than the other. Maybe that's why it was special.

Today was special, that's for sure, so much so that none of my notes seemed to pack the right punch. And I needed to keep track of my own history. After all, there was still the obligatory autobiography to write.

"I chose because I had no choice."

Maybe air quotes were necessary, just in case somebody famous had used that line before. And even if they hadn't, the President wouldn't know. He would assume it was a famous quotation, and he'd be scared to look uninformed.

I chose…because I had no choice. None whatsoever.

That's better. Drop the air quotes and sound more declarative. More in control. Presidents like that.

"So, you look deep in thought, there," the driver said. "Am I right? Huh? Can I read people or what?"

I sighed again. That was my response. But now, don't go and get the wrong idea about me. I don't like to be rude. It isn't in my nature. It really isn't. It's just that today I needed to chew over more important things than his Fruit Stripe gum.

"Hold on!" the driver shouted while squealing his brakes. "Dog crossed the road, or something."

I bobbed up and down for a moment, the belt tugging me towards a car seat that I wanted to escape. My eyes spied out the window, but I saw no dog, no "something." And from the sound of it, my new friend hadn't even swallowed his gum.

The President. *Mr.* President. That sounded good. And respectful, but then again, it bears repeating that the President asked to meet with me, not the other way around. And our meeting was monumental. One for the history books.

After all, this was the first time that any American President had hosted a serial killer in the White House.

Now that's something. That's really something.

CHAPTER 2

Collecting Dreams

Lee Harvey Oswald was a patsy. He said so, and it was true. I'm convinced of that fact, and, believe me, I've read enough books on the subject to prove it. It was back in grade school that the JFK assassination first gripped my imagination. Me and a friend named Andy drew pictures of the Texas Book Depository and Dealey Plaza and the brains splattering out of the back of the limo. Andy later ended up going into insurance claims. Hail damage and all that.

They say that about a thousand books have been published on the assassination. I'm not sure if that's true, but I personally own 514 of them. 'Course I don't own 514 *different* books, because I've bought a few favorites in both paperback and hardcover. Jack Ruby's brother even autographed one of them for me.

I'm proud of the collection, which I started when I was about eight or nine. That would have been in Oklahoma City. Good town. Good times, catterwalling around as a dumb kid. After I had bought my first twenty or thirty books on the assassination, I arranged them on a shelf in alphabetical order, by title rather than by author. I mean, who's ever even heard of these folks? Some of them are probably pen names anyway. The title: that's what counts.

By the end of high school, I had amassed enough JFK assassination books to display them by size. I started with the two tallest books on the left and right sides of the shelf.

Then the second tallest, and the third tallest, down to the very shortest in the middle. It created a nice visual effect. A valley, or a glen, as the Irish might say. For it to look perfect, I had to buy spare copies of a few books. I also had to throw out one that I sort of liked, but it didn't ride the visual wave, so it had to go.

As time went on, I couldn't resist purchasing more JFK books. Oliver Stone's movie meant that there were so many more of them. And their increasing numbers required a new filing system. In my first house, I built special shelves after tabulating all the common book sizes, from coffee table editions to pesky little paperbacks. Based upon their percentages, one could even try to predict the likely sizes of forthcoming releases, thus allowing adequate space for future growth.

All things being equal, I'll admit that it took me a long time to become as certain about my own life as I was about Oswald. That's the problem when you've got options. I was a good student, particularly at math and history and art. And I was good-looking. Well, average. Dark complexion and almost six feet tall. Nearly five-ten, anyhow. And my shock of brown hair waves real nice when I finger it with wet-look gel.

Maybe it was just the end result of green-eyed jealousy, but certain kids in high school didn't like me. And sometimes I'd join a clique that would later ostracize me, as if I wasn't as great as they first believed. Assholes, really, each and every one. That's what they were. This world's just silly with assholes.

The same kind of thing happened at my university. Some folks started out liking me, but then they got to where they didn't. Oh well. There were always other people. And when they turned on me too, I'd just move onto some more. Keep on the move. Keep on trucking.

No big deal, except that such movement framed my entire outlook on life, or so my psychiatrist tells me. Thinking about an old philosophy class, I recall that a lot of the best ways of looking at life are pretty simple when you get down to it. Not fortune cookie simple, maybe not even greeting card simple, but thirty-second TV commercial simple.

If I had to put it into words, my personal philosophy is that most people suck. They're cruel. They're hypocritical. And they're rude.

Most people, but not all. My parents were cool, but they both died way too young in a car wreck. The cops said it was Dad's fault, what happened, but I never believed them. But they left me the house and a chunk of money in the bank. Not much, but a kind of trust fund. It paid the bills and kept a college-guy lifestyle going long after college. I didn't have much, but I didn't have to work.

As for women, well, I've dated some great gals over the years. Half-crazy, a few of them, but they were basically cool, at least until they turned into assholes. Speed bumps on the road to somewhere better.

Some chicks can be downright difficult, which is why you've gotta have one or two stable friends on your side. Old pals, like Chet. We met at college. From a distance, I mistook him for a kid from my high school. Once we spoke, things kept going from there.

In most ways, the two of us are pretty different. Chet liked to joke that, if we weren't friends, then we'd never have become friends. But we had great times together, like all those trips to the multiplex. We were so broke that we'd share the same bucket of bottomless popcorn, trading it out at specific intervals during the movies. And there'd be a bunch of flicks because we'd stay all day, secretly roving from screen to screen.

Yeah, Chet was the coolest, a character-and-a-half. Wild man back in the day. Popular with the ladies, even though he was short and had reddish hair. Deep into comic books, and a super pothead. He was the main reason I intentionally took a fifth year to finish my degree, just so we could keep hanging out. But then Chet went to law school and got married and stopped partying. Somehow he became an Adult.

Despite my original plan, I decided not to get a degree in Letters. A lot of it would have been English classes, but, maybe more to the point, the name of that degree sounded pretty wussy. Everyone develops impressions of themselves that are or are not true, but I am quite confident that I'm not a wuss. At least, deep down inside I aspire to wusslessness.

That's why I got a degree in Communications. Strong enough for a man, but gentle enough for a woman. We've all got to talk sometimes, and everybody's always talking at us, so there you go. As for the real-world applications of that major, well, that remains an X factor.

Among other things, college helped me postpone Real Life, giving me a chance to consider the right career path. And the sad fact is that I just wanted to be famous. I didn't have any particular talent, but I longed for popularity, more than anything else. I wanted people to like me, but from a distance, so that I didn't really have to deal with them, certainly not on any level other than the surfacey kind. That was one reason.

But the main reason was, well, hell. Fame, just like the song says. I wanted to be well-known. If you go to wondering about why we're here, why we exist, fame seems to be the best answer to the great question, you know. And I have a birthright to notoriety, because of the American dream and all that stuff. I wanted to make my mark, to live forever. To be famous.

That's when I decided to murder somebody.

See, the way I figured it, and I did give this quite a bit of thought, if you want to be famous and you have no talent, you're best to go shooting at people. Maybe that sounds a tad extreme, but it really is the quickest way to get talked about in today's world.

To be honest, my first didn't go well for me. 'Nuff said. Then I shot a second victim in Albuquerque in 1999. Easy pickins. The boob never even saw it coming. But that was all part of my early work that has never been given proper attention. There was a short article about Victim Two in the *Albuquerque Journal* the day after, not much else.

And that goes to the real heart of the matter. No one ever stops to think about the hard work you have to put into becoming a serial killer. Particularly a successful serial killer. Like, you can't off someone you know personally, because that will eventually lead the authorities right to you. In fact, it's best not to kill strangers near where you live, either. Proximity is a distinct no-no.

You also don't want to kill too many people too quickly, as those same authorities will come under so much public pressure that they have to form entire units of detectives to catch you. You see, this is the kind of stuff that they don't teach you in school or put in books. Screw autobiographies. I should really write a manual: *The Idiot's Guide to Serial Killing,* or maybe a cute title like *In the Offing.*

The main point is that you can't be too conservative when it comes to this stuff. The Albuquerque murder was the work of a serial killer in the making, but not a serial killer. Serial means just that: a series. Say you want to be a serial killer, and you commit two great murders. Maybe you even get a lot of good press. But then you make the mistake of stepping out in front of a Mack truck. Game over, and not just for you, but also for your reputation. Two bodies do not a serial killer make. Not by a damn sight. You've gotta have at least three.

Style is another key factor. In today's world, killing people isn't enough because there are so many murders, most of them forgotten before they ever get known. So you have to carve out a unique persona. Don't sell the steak; sell the sizzle. That's why I originally considered being the Cereal Killer, leaving bowls of Cocoa Pebbles, Kaboom, and Boo Berry beside my victims. Or maybe just Life Cereal, in order to be ironic.

Later, I pondered becoming the Moustache Killer. It wasn't that I intended to murder people who had them. No, my plan was to draw moustaches on my victims once they were dead. I had a good track record of that during my childhood, pencilling all manner of facial hair inside of library books. That was along with wearing out more than one Wooly Willy.

At first I feared that I was going to have a Sharpie problem, but I solved it. You see, they mainly sell black Sharpies, especially at stores with limited stock. But a lot more people have brown hair than black, and therein lies the difficulty. Black and brown don't really go together. Two-tone is a fine thing, but it requires greater contrast. So I thought about buying Sharpies in bulk from a specialty store, one that sold them in green and blue and red and so forth.

Or maybe use oil paints instead, which really could have opened up a rainbow of possibilities. Together with a palette and brush, I would have been able to create moustaches carefully coordinated to match a victim's hair and clothing.

But in the end, I gave up on the idea. Becoming a serial killer takes determination and willpower. And if I'm totally honest about myself, I'm a procrastinator. In my twenties, there were lots of girls and parties and video games and music and movies and drugs and booze. Salad days, with lots and lots of dressing. The joys of youth. Life gets in the way. Yada, yada.

People tell me that dreams are good, and that nightmares are bad. But by the age of 37, I had finally come to understand the awful truth that dreams are scarier. Once they're deferred, dreams tend to mock their dreamers. You can try to banish them to the back of your mind, but they still end up loitering right square in the middle of your daily thoughts. Unfulfilled goals. Unfinished business.

Despite my laziness, I still desperately wanted to be famous, which automatically meant that I desperately wanted to be a serial killer. Laying the foundation of any career is tough, especially if you choose to be self-employed. If you choose because, well, because you have no choice.

Older and wiser, I did realize that the world wasn't quite ready for corpses sporting fuchsia and magenta moustaches. It was too overt, and too serious an attempt at wit.

And so, with new resolve to make my dreams finally come true, I waited for days and then weeks for a great idea to hit me. Inspiration. When that didn't happen, I took my Glock 9mm and my best knife on a road trip. The three of us went to Arizona. We'd improvise.

Making your mark is a tough thing to do in today's world. The sheer damn size of today's population makes that a fact. And dreams don't come true over night. At the outset, the stage where I stood was much larger than the size of my audience, and mathematically that ratio is screwed.

You see, that's why I knew Lee Harvey Oswald was a patsy. Oswald said he was. If he really had made one of the greatest hits of all time, he'd have wanted to take credit for it. He would've needed to take credit for it. The whole world was watching. Oswald had everyone's attention, but he calmly and clearly announced he wasn't the gunman.

You see, I could never lie about something so important. I'm much too good a person for that.

CHAPTER 3

Road Kill

"First time at the Hotel Congress?"

The clerk asked the question in such a way as to make it sound like a statement, like he'd already heard the answer before, and in fairness, he'd probably heard it plenty of times, day in and day out. I gave him a yes nod, and tuned out everything else he said. It was rote. The guy spoke in a monotone about ice buckets, sort of like the voice on an airplane that tells you what to do in an emergency. And his eyes looked dull, the bulbs behind them burning fairly dim.

Tucson is a good town. I wanted my first victim, at least my first new victim, to be in Tucson. Good Mexican food. Lots of history. Projecting ahead, I preferred to think that my memoirs would claim my serial killing began in Tucson.

It wasn't by mistake that I chose the Hotel Congress as a base. John Dillinger stayed there once. Now that was a criminal. The Great Depression and machine guns and old roadsters tearing down dirt roads. Bank robbing is a very different line of work than serial killing, but I have oodles of respect for it. Those guys weren't wusses. And all these years later, they're still famous. That's immortality for you.

If I let myself think about it too long, though, I get pissed off. Dillinger and Pretty Boy and Baby Face and all the rest, including their big city mafia counterparts, they had it easy. Sure, they got caught or killed. But they pulled their jobs back before modern security systems, before 24-hour television news, before DNA tests, and before every snot-nosed kid had a video camera on his snot-nosed smart phone.

Deep breaths, that's what my psychiatrist advises. Breathe in, and then breathe out, slowly, like I'm blowing up a big balloon, one colored sky blue. Go to a happy place. After all, I couldn't afford to get all riled up for two reasons. One was that the Congress was a nice place. It still had the old wooden mailboxes behind the front desk, and real room keys, not those credit card-style wannabes. The whole place was stuck in the thirties, just like when Dillinger stayed there. That included the rooms, which had radios instead of televisions. Great for late-night Ghost-to-Ghost, unreality radio instead of reality TV.

I also wanted to be happy because I was supposed to be happy. There I was in Arizona, Making Things Happen. It was the dawn of a new day in my life. I was staking out a real career, and I was damn sure going to become famous this time. 'Course I'd probably have to send little messages to the press in the tradition of Zodiac Killer puzzles and anagrams and so forth. Inscrutable codes. Signs and tokens, even. I remember reading that phrase in a Dickens novel back in high school. Signs and tokens. Not arcade tokens, but the old school meaning. *Tokens.*

Yeah, there was every reason to be happy. And who wants to be pissed off while murdering somebody? That said, you can't get crazy ecstatic, either, like all laughing and giggling, or people would go and think that you're damned zany. The newspapers would label you with some ridiculous moniker like Joy Boy. The Joy Boy Killer. The Joy Boy Murders. Lord have mercy.

But see, that's where the planning comes in. If you want to seem way cool, and if you want a good serial killer pseudonym, you have to construct things in such a way as to lead the press to water. That made me snicker. A horse will find its way to water, I thought, but a pencil must be lead. Good joke. Clean, too. Not like all that dirty stuff today. Hard to believe what the networks can get away with. Insanity has truly found its way to TV screens, and you know, the parents nowadays just don't care. They really don't.

I sat on the chair in the hotel room drinking a bottle of peach tea while contemplating the failure of the modern American family. In my youth, I never saw the kind of trash kids watch today. And if I looked at something naughty, like a lingerie catalog, I knew it was naughty, because I'd have to sneak a peak and then feel guilty afterwards, not at all like internet porn. But people today. My god a-mighty. The death of modern civilization.

I unpacked, taking my pet rock Frog out of my pocket and gently resting him beside the radio. Frog was cool. Every so often, I had to touch up his eyes and mouth with a magic marker, but that was cool too, because it gave me a chance to alter his expression and give him a new look. Someday I might even give him a moustache. Pet rocks rock.

After I sat Frog down, I immediately picked him back up, like all-of-a-sudden. In fact, I repacked everything and went back downstairs. Something told me that it had come time for action.

As soon as I shot the clerk once in each of his eyes, I knew right then and there that I had made a good decision. It had all come to me in a flash. Three murders that collectively would lead the press to one and only one clear conclusion. And the first went off like a charm.

Nobody was in the lobby when I pulled the trigger. The clerk hardly knew it happened. That's how little attention he was paying. He must have seen my gun, even if it was at the last second. But he was non-plussed, like he didn't care. He fell to the floor after the first bullet hit his left eye, which made it easy to fire the second shot into his right.

I thought about Dillinger again while exiting the Congress. The police nabbed him there. But here I was, walking calmly out of the place with no cops in sight. *Sight.* Now, that's a funny joke, and clean too.

Of course, someone must have heard the gunfire, and so someone must have dialed 9-11. Phoned 9-11. *Phoned* 9-11! Because no one actually *dials* the numbers anymore. Things really do suck in today's world. I miss sticking my finger in the dial, and particularly miss hearing it spin back into position on its own speed. Anyhow, the responding officers would find the body soon enough, but by that time I would be long gone.

Next came the old dude in Mesa. He was sitting near the fountain at the Superstition Springs Center. I insisted to myself that the second victim should be an Everyman, and he was that. Pretty blah, pretty forgettable, and, well, pretty ugly.

The Adam's apple on this fella was something to behold. No one can be good-looking and have an Adam's apple like that. I sat down beside him, but the guy said nothing. Perfect. He was quiet, him and his apple. My god, it was like you could cut it out, throw it over to Eve, and let her chow down. And she would, too, that bitch.

Just before closing time, I followed the old dude out of the mall. It was starting to get dark. He walked slowly, one leg limping a bit, a hitch in his get-along. That made it easy for me to sprint over to my truck, start it, and then drive right beside him. Old dude looked at me, slowly, without saying a word. His apple didn't even gulp. This really was perfect.

After my bullet hit him at such close range, his frail old body moved faster than it probably had in years. I sure didn't miss. One shot right square in the mouth.

This time I heard the sirens, and while I was still in the parking lot, waiting to pull out onto the main road. I worried as to whether the joint had security cameras. Come to think of it, shopping malls probably aren't the smartest places to kill folks. On the one hand, I was hiding in plain sight. On the other hand, I was hiding in plain sight.

Keep moving, I ordered myself, once the mall appeared in my rear view mirror. But not too slow. The speed of a getaway car requires a careful tightrope act like the type a drunk driver has to perform. If you go too slow, you might attract attention. But you can't go too fast either. Just right. Play it cool. Joe Cool.

Spotting a gas station hours later in Phoenix, I pulled over to get my bearings. I hate maps, not because I don't understand them, but because I can't ever get them to fold back up properly. I always have to force some of the creases to go the wrong way. Hearing another siren, I got a little worried. More than a little worried, with hot air building up inside my chest. But the cop car passed me without so much as a glance. Deep breaths, in and out, in and out. Made me wonder if the Prozac was working, or if the pharmacy was running some cheap generic on me.

Go west, pet rock. I figured California should be the next destination. Years earlier, me and Chet had taken a trip to Venice Beach. Crazy, crazy fun. Hot chicks and some guy on roller skates strumming an electric guitar. Good times had by all. We smelled pot, but we didn't toke any. And we didn't get near any of those babes either, but we sure enjoyed the second-hand smoke from the whole scene. It wafted our way real nice thanks to that cool Pacific breeze.

For no particular reason, I figured that I'd do my final victim in the early morning hours. Victorville was nice. Nothing too distinctive about it, but it was nice. After a couple days of scouting and, frankly, procrastinating, I got itchy. The longer I was gone from Oklahoma, the harder it would be to concoct an alibi. On the phone, I told Chet that I was in Padre, but I'd have hard a time proving that in court of law, especially since I'd never been to Padre.

Eventually, I spotted a woman on the side of the road. It wasn't very long after sunup, and the air had a slight chill in it. From a distance, she seemed attractive, but as I got closer and closer, she looked older and older. Lots of wrinkles, probably from years of smoking cigarettes. I had known a guy who worked for big tobacco once. Horrible character, the type that thought he was cute, but was just another ass. How many people have suffered because of those jerks? There's so much unnecessary grief and misery in this world. It'd drive you to hazard if you let it.

Anyhow, the gal's car was broken down. Steam rose from the engine. It was a white T-Bird, one of those late eighties models. I pulled over, offering to help. She was on the verge of tears, which made me feel more than a bit sorry for her. I'm a sucker for a lady in distress.

"Motherfucker palmed a lemon on me."

"Well, you sure can't trust used car dealers."

"This one was supposed to be a friend of mine. He took my cash to an auction."

"All the cars at auctions have problems. That's why they're there."

"I should've known not to trust him."

Our verbal exchange was rapidly giving birth to a conversation. And the temperature outside was rising. Or maybe it was just heating up inside my body again. Sweat beaded on my forehead while she kept right on yapping.

All I could think about was the 9mm just beneath my leather coat. My holster resembled the one McQueen wore in *Bullitt,* which was based on the one used by the San Francisco cop who chased the Zodiac killer. After looking up and down the road and seeing that we were alone, I took several steps back to my truck. Then I mouthed a lengthy sentence to her.

"What?"

I mouthed another sentence. Gobbledygook.

"What?"

When I started running for her, I grabbed my pistol like it was a knife. I might have yelled something, but to be honest, I don't remember. By the time she cottoned on, it was too late. Blood ran from both of her ears.

Like so many of the world's best ideas, my plan was deceptively simple. Three bodies in rapid succession. They used to say that all kinds of things come in threes, magic things, including the deaths of famous people. And one thing was for sure, these three deaths added up to a series.

And it had a clear, concise meaning: See No Evil, Speak No Evil, Hear No Evil. Easy to interpret, and short enough for newspaper headlines. Some of the pointy-heads would probably say it had relevance to the times in which we lived. Maybe they'd even use the word *zeitgeist.*

But then came massive disappointment in the form of, well, nothing. No headlines were published. It was like a cruel repeat of my old Albuquerque hit. Brief mention of the three individual murders appeared in local newspapers, but no one made the connection between them. I checked, over and over again, even bothering to go online, something that I dearly hate doing.

The journalists couldn't draw the lines between the three murders and see the constellation they formed. All those ancient people looked up at the night sky and drew imaginary lines between stars, usually creating overly complicated pictures of mythical gods and heroes and crap. But the feet-on-the-desk media were clearly asleep at the wheel when it came to my work, or they didn't have a lick of sense.

In Culver City, I went into a cheap bar and sank into a booth with red leatherette seats, just me and Frog and a rum and a coke. What didn't work? What kept my message from penetrating the market place? Why couldn't I cut through the noise? There I was breaking my back and the world just sighed. I'd been ho-hummed in no uncertain terms.

Maybe I should have offed all three victims in the same town, or at least the same state. And maybe I should have used a knife on the eyes, ears, and mouth. That would have been more graphic, and it would have made for better pictures, even if they were blurred out on the evening news. That's important, clearly. Lesson learned. But how exactly does one cut out a mouth, especially if you want to avoid comparisons to the Joker?

Were spontaneity and planning truly at odds, or could they work together? Now there's a question for a Letters major. Of course, after the third rum, everyone's a philosopher. And by the fourth, at least when you're 37, you just want to go to bed, knowing all the while that you won't be able to sleep through the night, no matter how much you've drunk. Not at that age. You'll have to get up to pee at least once.

Driving back to Oklahoma City, I thought and thought and thought. Then I stopped at a Dairy Queen, had an Orange Julius, which wasn't as good as it should have been, incidentally, not like the old days when they used to taste good, and then I thought and thought and thought. I dug on some Joe Cocker and listened to some talk radio and then I thought some more.

But no answers came.

CHAPTER 4

The Fat Man

I didn't know if it was okay to laugh when the fat guy fell on his face, you know, whether that would be P.C. in today's world. At the starting gate, let it be known that I did not shoot him in the back. That would not have been cool. No sir. I shot him in the side of the head. Well, the back-of-the-side-of-the-head. And I used a silencer to do it. Cost me over $400. Maybe that was cheating, but who cares.

The guy was bald, except for a little semi-circle of hair over his ears, just enough to remind his cranium of all that had been lost during the battle of life. He grunted something when his body swallowed the bullet. I couldn't hear too well because I was several feet away at the time. Maybe that was cheating too.

He might have said, "You Shot Me." Now that would've been funny. Seems like somebody famous actually did say that once. 'Course the fat man may have just choked on blood or experienced some kind of motor reflex. Come to think of it, it was more of a gurgle than a grunt. I love it in the old cartoons when Bugs or Daffy drink something and you hear the actual words "Gurgle, Gurgle, Gurgle" instead of sound effects.

Nice clothes, though. I dress casual, but I admire guys like the Fat Man who sport nice duds. Expensive suit and shoes. He was probably wearing cufflinks too, but once I'd taken the starch out of him, I didn't have time to look.

Will Rogers World Airport was never particularly busy. They call it a "world" airport because no international flights depart from Oklahoma City, but they still want it to sound kinda-sorta international. Perhaps the stranger thing was the fact that the airport was named after a guy who died in a plane crash. Anyways, few flights arrived or departed after 10 PM. That's one reason the Fat Man was a safe choice.

Sure, I was against killing people near my home, but airports are a little different. They're like how bus and train stations used to be. They might be located in particular cities, but they're a nether region full of travellers, full of people coming and going, full of people who aren't there yet. A bit like purgatory.

The Fat Man was on his way somewhere, and, thanks to me, he was on his way somewhere else. Maybe that's a good thing. Maybe his wife hated him or maybe he was going bankrupt or so on and so forth. Lots of troubles and no future. He hadn't planned to die today anymore than I had planned to shoot him.

Driving back to my house, I considered how important it is to be spontaneous sometimes. At the last second, I wheeled into a Sonic drive-in without thinking about it. "Large cherry limeade and tater tots," I barked.

"Is that all for ya?" the Speaker replied.

"Yeah. No, wait. Wait. Give me a grilled chicken sandwich too."

"That'll be $8.27. We'll have it right out."

The Speaker was honest as the day is long. The drink and bag of food appeared in mere seconds. I started to ask for ketchup, but held my tongue. Nine bucks. Keep the change.

Instead of eating there, I took the food to go. All the while I was reminded of the time that me and Chet were in Vegas. We couldn't find our way out of Caesar's Palace, so we kept gambling, trying different games. Slots, Blackjack, Roulette. The only difference was that this time I was confident that I wasn't going to burn alive. That's what kept going through my mind at Caesar's. You see, if a fire starts in a Vegas casino, probably everyone would burn to death. Those places are designed to keep you inside, to keep you gambling. It's like they don't have exit signs, unless somehow in an emergency they descend from the ceiling and start blinking. 'Course smoke inhalation and trampling would take most of the gamblers out, not the flames.

It was around 4 AM that I woke up on my couch. I actually prefer the word "sofa," but don't use it much in conversation because I don't wanna come across like a wuss. Once I even thought about buying a chaise lounge. The clerk at the store in Oklahoma City corrected me, saying chaise "lounge." He emphasized the "lounge" part to sound superior. Maybe he was dyslexic, or maybe he was just arrogant, but correcting pronunciations really is the first and last defense of the fool. Funny thing is, the chick I was dating at the time agreed with him. You just never can tell about some people.

I often fall asleep on the couch in front of the TV set, so much so that the middle cushion has developed a permanent indentation from my ass. To any Sherlock stopping by, it would have been apparent where things had gone down that night. A wad of foil on the floor cradled the remains of the rubbery chicken, but the tots were long gone. I'd feasted while nodding off to the news.

Attention Deficit Disorder was never something I believed in until cable news transformed around the turn of the millennia. Instead of just being 24 hours a day, seven days a week, the news became a wild assault on the senses. An anchor yaps about stuff while constant text about other subjects bombards the viewer on the right and left of the screen and on the ticker tape below. That was all in addition to the station identification logo, a clock, and the occasional weather map.

But there are rare moments when the stars align. Once my eyes adjusted, I realized that the anchor and text and ticker tape all spoke about the same story. Brewster Jameson was dead. Somewhere in the windmills of my mind I remembered that name. Maybe he was a bigshot businessman or something.

Jameson's file photo and footage of him shaking hands with politicians didn't look familiar, but then I saw the back of his head. Well, the back-of-the-side-of-the-head. Good god. Jameson was the Fat Man at the airport. The Fat Man at the airport was Jameson. The two fat men were one and the same.

There he was, lying on the ground in a bigger pool of blood than I remembered. Had someone else shot him too? No, wait. He must have bled a lot more while I was at the Sonic. And blood on asphalt is probably like motor oil. A little bit of oil looks like a lot more than it is. That worries some drivers.

Still groggy, I changed the channel. I had stumbled to the television to get the remote, stumbled back to the couch, and squinted to find the right button. Of course it was hardly a button, just a tiny piece of rubber. All of a sudden, I recalled the wonderful noise the old TV knobs used to make when you turned them. Great sounds. Bump, bump, bump. That was the VHF knob. Bump, bump, bump. Of course the UHF knob went click, click, click. A bit more dainty, like it was the woman of the two.

Surfing channels, I stopped on the World News Broadcasting. WNB, they called it in a deep voice on the promos. The guy would say WNB, and then there were three quick laser beam sounds. *Bzzuu, bzzuu, bzzz-zuuuu.* The third one lasted the longest. They also had better graphics than the other news stations. Stuff flew at the screen all the time, almost like 3-D, but not quite.

WNB aired some footage of ambulance guys putting Brewster's body onto a stretcher. They tried to cover him, but the sheet billowed in the wind, and I noticed how bad his head really looked. It was a sight to see. Hopefully his family would be smart and do the dignified, closed-casket thing. Then again, some morticians are really artists. And they don't get the credit they deserve in this life.

I left the front room to boil some hot water in the microwave. I love plain hot water unspoiled by tea bags or anything else. Funny, but I never have liked cold water, preferring soda pop or iced tea. Hot water does the trick, though. Cuts through the phlegm.

Surprisingly, WNB stayed focused on Jameson's death. In short order, they featured a series of clips with a baritone voice recounting all of his many accomplishments.

"Brewster Jameson has been well known in this country since his days as a campus radical in the sixties. Extremely controversial at times, Jameson fought on behalf of far left-wing causes throughout his career."

The sixties, wow. From the back-of-the-side-of-his-head, Jameson didn't look quite that old.

Within minutes, the story had a name. *Political Assassination in the Heartland.* It was written in a great font. *Heartland* had little cracks all over it, like there had been an earthquake or something. If this kept up, they'd probably add one or two ominous music notes behind the title graphic. Or maybe laser guns. *Bzzzzuuuu.*

"The assassin was clearly a right-wing lunatic," one pundit declared.

"No, no," another argued. "He was most likely a left-winger upset with Jameson, who had become a sell-out. In recent years, he was nothing more than a middle-of-the-road moderate. Something of a D.L.C. Democrat."

A parade of other experts dissected the intense amount of planning that must have gone into the operation. They debated as to whether the shooter had stalked Jameson city-by-city. Maybe he was even an assassin hired by a foreign power or was part of a cartel of killers. Like Murder, Inc., I thought.

But then I dwelled on the fact that I was not an assassin. Maybe all assassins are murderers, but all murderers aren't assassins. That's a different kettle of fish entirely. And of course all murderers aren't serial killers either, and that's where all of this was starting to go wrong. The Fat Man had just been a way to blow off steam. Target practice during a lull, a period in which to regroup and reconnoiter. None of this assassin talk made any sense.

Maybe I'm a patsy, I thought.

Then I watched more TV.

CHAPTER 5

Wise Up

Robert Lynch psyched himself up for the next segment of his live television program. It was like method acting, he once told himself in complete confidence. Sometimes you have to get the old face beat red in order to show folks how angry you are. And sometimes you need to well up the eyes. You can't cry. If you do, you lose all respect. But the appearance of touchy-feeliness can look powerful. Threatening to cry without doing it.

Robert was no pushover, certainly not to the seventeen million viewers who watched him faithfully. Five days a week, he fought the left-wing tooth and nail. Social programs, family values, defense budgets: the whole enchilada.

And every great once in a while, he railed against the right-wing too. Tab Hudson, his producer, had originally given him that idea. It helped spark controversy, which was always a good way to resuscitate the ratings. To be perfectly honest, not all seventeen million viewers did watch him faithfully. Sometimes a few million or more strayed. Robert would get into a rut, harping on the same issue for weeks at a time, and boredom took hold out in TV Land.

Squabbling with right-wingers a few times a year was good for business. It made Robert look reasonable. Libertarians liked it, and they were His People. That was to say nothing of all the news programs on WNB and the other stations. On his own show, Robert was a commentator, but the other twenty-three hours of the day, the press commented on him. The news revolved around the news. To think.

Sometimes Robert thought about thinking, but usually he didn't bother. His bestselling children's book was an updated version of *The Little Train that Could,* which he touted as his autobiography, one fit for everybody to read. None of that intellectual malarkey. Robert was a steam engine who choo-chooed his way across America. Anything that stood in his way didn't stand in his way, including his coworkers, who loathed him.

Of course no matter how powerful they are, trains have to run on tracks, and Robert had a one-track mind. Get viewers, and keep them. That was why it was time for a bit of emotion.

The red light appeared on the camera positioned in front of his desk. Robert began by looking down, his right hand stroking his forehead. Then he took a deep, solemn breath, exhaled dramatically, and stared right into the audience's eyes.

"You know, America, a lot of time has been spent talking about *Me* again, and what I really want to talk about is *You.* Each one of *You. All of You. You* are the reason *I'm* here, but *They* don't like that. They want to hurt *You* by getting at *Me. They* want to derail the Robert Lynch Express."

At that point, the green-screened graphics behind Robert shifted from nondescript geometric shapes to an enormous American flag waving in the wind. Being fake was so much easier than having a real set.

Robert took another deep breath, making a whistle-like sound when he blew it out.

"Well, they can't. And they won't."

He looked down, shaking his head. Then he looked directly into the camera again.

"Yes, I made money from Oceanic Banking stock, and yes I gave speeches at some of their gatherings. But let's be clear. All the money I ever received from Oceanic has been donated to charities. The full list is on the website, folks. It's all there. We have nothing to hide. I...have absolutely nothing to hide."

Robert's voice deepened considerably when he spoke that last sentence. Then he stopped speaking. He looked up, solemnly, as if staring towards a higher power. Cue commercial break. Time to sell soap.

Robert stood up and stretched. He liked to stretch, but not to exercise. The paunch of old was the fat of new. These days, suspenders replaced belts.

Tab briefly congratulated Robert, suggesting that he should downplay the next segment. The charity remark was the soundbite of the day. It was the one that other programs would replay. It didn't matter that no credible news organization had really spent time talking about the invented controversy before. They would now, and all to the greater good.

All that was left to report was the Brewster Jameson story. File footage was ready to go. Mention his death. Talk about the left-wing causes he supported. And then roll credits on Episode 1,059 of *Wise Up, America!*

Robert stood up for the final segment. The old footage showed Jameson standing, and Robert was not about to be overshadowed.

As usual, Robert winged most of what he said. He covered the basics, and added that his own coverage of Jameson had made the aging liberal radioactive among the Normal Folks and the Good People.

"Wise Up, America! Brewster Jameson was an enemy of the state. He was Our Enemy. And let's be grownups here. Let's be reasonable, and let's be honest.

Sometimes…yes, I know it sounds funny at first…but sometimes assassins are heroes."

Robert paused long enough to stroke his chin once.

"If Hitler had been assassinated, we'd call the person who did it a hero. Right? Don't you see what this is all about? Don't you see? Don't you see what this is all really and truly about, America?"

Tab was worried, for the first time in quite awhile. Robert shot from the hip. All he needed was a full pot of coffee each day, maybe a pot and a half, or even two. No cue cards. Just enough coffee to stoke the old steam engine.

Usually it worked. Tab always believed that viewers could sense Robert wasn't speaking from prepared notes or from a teleprompter. It was part of what made him seem genuine. And if someone seems authentic, then they are authentic.

But Tab never forgot Program 47, when Robert called the President a state-sponsored terrorist. That caused a huge backlash, even if it helped transform a small audience into an enormous one. Or Program 473, when he announced with certainty that Belgium was America's true enemy. Or Program 855, when he exposed the secret that Neo-Nazis in the Red Cross planned to erect a statue of Herman Goering in Kansas.

Robert frequently invoked religion as well. On Program 226, he lectured viewers on the fermentation of wine, demanding that all copies of the Holy Bible be rewritten to replace the word "wine" with "juice." He claimed that Jesus really didn't make wine, because that was alcohol and it was immoral to drink. Jesus surely wouldn't be trying to get folks liquored up. Even still, many preachers got irritated when he suggested that everyone tear out pages mentioning "wine" in any edition that didn't tell the Truth.

Normally the Robert Lynch Express stayed on track. And on track meant going the distance and then some. Further than anyone else. That was the gimmick. That was the knockout punch. Other commentators were scared to go as far. And they were scared of Robert, too.

Nevertheless, Tab knew that going too far was a very different thing than going way, way too far. A few people picketing outside their building was good for business. That's what you want, really, along with some nasty editorials in snobby newspapers and liberal rags.

If all of these things went through Tab's mind in the space of an instant, it was because he had thought about them so many times before. After all, Tab believed in winding audiences down after winding them up. Tab believed in being strategic about detonating bombs. Tab knew, or at least believed that he knew, when to rein it in. But he wasn't so sure about Robert, who kept ranting.

"I'm telling you, America. The man who did this to Brewster Jameson may have been an assassin, but he is no murderer."

Robert shrugged his shoulders and nodded his head ever so slightly, as if he was shaking off an unthinkable thought. Then he inhaled again, which always helped him change tempo. It was a good transition.

"This assassin is not a criminal to hate, but a hero to celebrate. And I mean that, America. Lord in Heaven, I do mean that, as much as any words that I have ever spoken on this mortal coil."

Robert realized he had about seventy seconds left before the end of the program. He felt a surge go through him. At that moment, he was aware of every fibre in his body. He knew the right inflection to use and the right duration for every pause.

"Follow me now, America. Follow me. Walk with me. Walk in my shoes."

Those words preceded his impromptu movements around the set. He liked having the camera on the jib arm move with him. They were synchronous. They were together.

That's when he did the jig.

"See this America? See this? This is Brewster Jameson's grave, and I'm dancing on it. I'm dancing on it. Won't you dance with me? Come dance with me, America."

Tab's face went pale. His jaw fell open.

"I am saying to you, right now, officially, that I am the president of this assassin's fan club. Excuse me, this *hero's* fan club. Oh, sure, the pinkos will say I'm cruel. The pinkos will say I'm crazy. They'll lie and use some dirty word like murderer."

When he said that last word, he put his hands to both sides of his head. His fingers made air quotes.

"But let me speak directly to those left-wing wimps — and that's what they are people, wimps — for a moment."

That line was another clue. When he turned his head sharply to the side, the director switched to a different camera.

"You pinkos are the murderers of our country. You are the assassins of our freedoms and our morals and our values."

Robert looked up and sighed. It was a good effect, and it also gave him a chance to glance at the clock and calculate how many seconds he had left.

"But this man. This great man who eliminated Brewster Jameson has heard the call to arms. He has come to our rescue. He has come to us as a hero in the night against all odds. Brewster Jameson was an enemy of the people, and this hero — because now, from this moment forward, I will indeed refuse to call him an assassin — this hero followed in the hallowed path of our forefathers and eliminated an enemy of the people. This hero is truly a great man, and wherever he is today, I wish him…Godspeed."

Robert's voice went very low when he said "Godspeed."Then he walked back to his desk, sat down in his chair, and bid America goodnight. As always, the lights dimmed slowly as the closing theme played. Robert became a lone, silhouetted figure until he was replaced onscreen by a commercial for cowboy catheters.

It was only then that Tab remembered to breathe. Once he did, he realized that Robert's comments were already making news on other stations.

CHAPTER 6

Cosmology

Pizza boxes buried the remains of the Sonic grilled chicken. And my unshaven face hid my acne, at least to a degree. I hadn't moved in 24 hours. The TV glowed brighter than it ever had before.

Quite a few politicians decried *Wise Up, America!* Some people demanded the show be canceled. Lots of other folks plain didn't hear about the controversy, paying attention to the news that wasn't on the News. But then there were thousands and thousands, millions even, who agreed wholeheartedly with every single word that Robert Lynch had spoken.

A number of commentators and self-described journalists echoed his sentiments. A few went even further. Apparently a guy on AM Radio decreed that the headshot was too good for the likes of Brewster Jameson. The assassin should have used a bigger gun, he argued, one that would have exploded his left-wing brains all over the pavement.

Hiding at home, I wondered who was in charge. Was Robert Lynch the maestro, directing an orchestra of crazy musicians, or was he the person at the back of the line who could stand up on his tippy toes and see where some of the country was already heading?

A group of Robert's fans appeared at Brewster's funeral holding signs like "Jameson Was a Traitor!" and "Pinkos Die!" One of them copied Robert's dance from TV. Two others poured several gallons of water on the ground and dragged a Jameson effigy through the mud. Make no mistake about it. The Fat Man was unpopular.

When the police arrived at the memorial, they just observed the show. They also watched Jameson's relatives cry and cry and cry. No one seemed to care. 'Course I cared. I thought about phoning 1-800-Flowers.

After all, I never have been an ideological kind of guy. You see, I always vote for the man, not the party. Each election season, I suffer quietly through the campaign commercials, just like I do through PBS fundraising drives. And then the least bad candidate gets my vote. Except for the times I don't bother to vote.

How do I choose who is the least bad? Well-dressed and confident-talking types rise to the top of my list. And the person with the least number of scandals. They all have some baggage, so the real question is whose could qualify as a carry-on at the airport.

Middle-of-the-Road. That's me. That's Birch Barr. Of course, if you really are standing in the middle of the road you can get hit from both directions. I didn't know if I had read that in a book, or if I had made that up myself. I scratched it down on a scrap of paper just in case.

When I finally took a hot shower, I kept thinking about everything. The Prell lathered up and got in my eyes, stinging them. But I could still see. Maybe great things do happen to people sometimes. One little thing triggers everything you want, all at once. And sure as shooting, you have to Go For It.

After all, I had waited and waited and then tried and tried to become a serial killer. No luck, not with all my hard work. Then a spontaneous act created a chain reaction. Fate + Planning = Success. You could put that formula in a self-help book. It made sense. A lot of sense. Wise Up, America.

I shaved and dressed and then checked my credit card balance. I was going to need plenty of gas and a few more bullets. One murder does not a serial killer make.

A few days later, I stopped for a steak in Kansas City after shooting Cosmo Harrogate. I ordered it well done, but it came out medium.

It wasn't until I read back through several of Robert's blogs and program transcripts that I learned that Cosmo was a Very Bad Man. A British Ex-Pat who raised buckets of money for left-wing politicians. For most of his life in America, the guy was on deep background, or at least out of the public eye. No one knew or cared who he was, not until Robert exposed him on TV, day after day.

Footage of Cosmo made clear he was a wuss. A prissy wuss with bushy hair that would get all matted with blood after one bullet in the back-of-the-side-of-the-head. Wise up, England.

Finding him was easy enough. Cars lined the streets near the private mansion where the fundraiser took place. I sat for a few hours, imagining the ritzy types who met that day to throw money at liberal candidates.

After Cosmo emerged, he kept smiling and shaking hands. Get in the car. Go. Go. Come on, already. Go. But Cosmo kept smiling and waving like he was some kind of effeminate epileptic. Get in the car. Get in the car. Go. Go. For God's sake, man. Just go.

I turned the key and started my truck at the exact moment that Cosmo shut the door on his Benz. Was it the new model? Probably. The Ultimate Driving Machine. No, wait, that's BMW.

After a short drive, Cosmo's car finally pulled up to the Hyatt Regency at the Crown Center. Very nice. Lots of high-end restaurants. Hallmark has its world head-quarters somewhere near there, but they probably don't make greeting cards for occasions like this.

I went inside and tried to look normal. I spotted my mark at the hotel bar and took a seat nearby.

"Can I get you something, sir?" the waitress asked.

"Sure," I replied. "A beer would be nice."

"What kind?"

"The coldest you've got."

"Sure thing, honey bun."

She was slow about bringing the brewski, but it didn't matter, because Cosmo was even slower about drinking his whiskey or whatever it was. Probably sherry, the little weirdo.

To be honest, I began to worry that I'd have to go pee before Cosmo. I was much younger, so surely Cosmo would have to go first. Old British guys probably can't hold it for very long. But then again, a little glass of spirits doesn't take up as much bladder as a tall beer. I kept drinking, though, because I didn't have a newspaper. I had to do something with my hands.

I tried not to think about it, but it occurred to me how much the color of beer resembles urine. God, I should have asked for nachos and nothing to drink at all. I don't mind eating without a drink. It isn't difficult, unless the food is really doughy.

That floury taste means you have to smack your lips a lot.

Cosmo's drink was stationary. Half full. His cell phone rang, and he started chattering in that foreigner accent of his, and he didn't drink at the pauses because he didn't seem to take pauses. The guy on the other end of the line must have been a good listener. 'Course it really wasn't a *line,* anymore, I thought wistfully. Cosmo was on a cell phone. And there was no line, no wire, no cord.

"Just take care of it," Cosmo demanded before ending the call. His chin kind of leaned downward into the left side of his neck when he gave orders.

Standing up, Cosmo threw some bills onto the table. Then he charged off with a determination that made clear he knew where he was going. He left half his drink, so apparently he never planned to finish it. Maybe it wasn't any good.

I eyeballed his movements and then mimicked the same, pretending to be underwater, all calm-like, so as to not arouse suspicion while slow-trailing him. Cosmo did need to piss, and he had evidently pissed at the hotel before, because he sure knew his way to the men's room.

Pushing the door open, I found Cosmo preening himself in front of the mirror. Gee, I thought, this guy must pee really quick. Is his bladder so small that he only had a tiny bit of urine? Or did the wily old Brit not pee at all? Maybe he can hold it for a long time.

At a glance, I noticed that it was a very nice, clean restroom. Inside the stall, I drew my gun, screwed on the silencer, and then held it behind my back. Using a few squares of toilet paper, I opened the stall door with my left hand. When you get right down to it, public restrooms are hotbeds of germs and disease, even if they look clean.

I was just about to outstretch my right arm when Cosmo finished drying his hands and turned around. Damn. To make sure everyone knew that this was Victim Two, I had to give it to Cosmo in the back-of-the-side-of-the-head. So I decided to reveal the gun and give him to know my intentions.

"Would you please walk over to that dryer and turn your back to me?"

"What in God's name? I should say not."

"Turn around, fella. Turn around, or I'll shoot you square in the face."

"I prefer to scream."

"I'm telling you. Don't do it."

"Would you rather I stand and fight?"

"Instead of what? Screaming like a wuss? Just turn around."

Cosmo had balls, even if he was English. Him and his peculiar bladder lunged forward, challenging me on my own turf.

Leave it to this guy to screw things up. I squeezed the trigger extra hard, hoping that would make the bullet hit him even harder. Yeah, he went down, and nobody was any the wiser, at least not yet. But Cosmo had been shot in his chest. The back-of-the-side-of-his-head remained immaculate.

So I did the only reasonable thing I could. I turned Cosmo over. Then I stood down on the tile floor several feet away, leaning over a bit to get the right angle. That was when I noticed that either his head or his body looked all wrong. It was as if the fall forced his ear to shift upwards. Shit fire and save the damn matches.

Walking back over to him, I learned the real cause of Cosmo's trouble. Seems that he wore a toupee, which had gone all cock-eyed. After tugging it back into place, or the next closest thing, I aimed for the right spot and pulled the trigger again. Fuck a duck.

He had it coming, but the whole scene didn't feel quite right. Talking to the guy, and then having to shoot him in the wrong spot. And then cursing. I really prefer not to curse, even though I do on occasion.

After all, I didn't want to be profane.

I just wanted to be noteworthy.

CHAPTER 7

Treason

"I don't know how you did it, or why it's working," Tab admitted while sitting in Robert's office. In the old days, the duo had usually met in Tab's office, but that all changed once their show became a hit.

It was early morning, and Tab was already tired. His ears stuck out a good bit from his head, but it felt like the one on the right didn't anymore. He had spent hours and hours pressing it against a phone since Robert did the Jameson jig on national TV. That ear was also hotter than the rest of his body.

WNB pollsters had been quick to determine what the Average Joe thought about Robert's endorsement of Brewster Jameson's murder. Right around thirty percent gave a big thumbs up, and another 25 percent were unaware who Jameson was or that he had taken a bullet.

That's not to say there weren't major complaints. There were always complaints. Liberal activists hated Robert with a passion. Four years ago, they skewered him when they learned that he'd lied about receiving a big broadcasting award. A couple of years later, they cheered when Robert's first wife Teresa wrote a book that claimed he was impotent. *Slow Below,* she called that chapter. It was the only part that anybody read.

Tab understood that liberal enemies were really good friends. Disparaging a firebrand like Robert helped turn him into a trademarked brand. Bad press is good press. And the by-product is that getting attacked inspires your fans to spring to your defense.

But the Jameson story was different. In one poll, a majority of women said that Robert was too harsh. Easily remedied, Tab thought. For the next week, we'll only book female guests. Maybe a pretty one, but better still if most of them look plain and talk plain. Tab texted his assistant: "Mid age fat w glasses."

Then there were some preachers and priests and even a rabbi who had appeared at a roundtable debate on a rival news network. Except that there was no debate. They agreed that Americans shouldn't be happy because a political figure had been murdered. After all, it wasn't as if Jameson was another Mussolini.

Along with cover from sensitive women, *Wise Up, America!* needed a tiny bit of cover from God. Not a problem. Tab kept a list of some fire-and-brimstone types who would agree with anything Robert said. Get them out onto the other WNB news shows to spout some harsh Old Testament stuff.

Tab's favorite phrase for political cover was "Pink Insulation." Years earlier, when Robert was getting started, he always snickered when Tab said that. Later, after he became successful, Robert argued that it should really be "Pinko Insulation," but Tab didn't budge. His victories were small and few in number, which made them count all the more.

The only other key group to complain were liberal politicians, but Tab paid no attention to them. WNB kept a few tired old liberals on the payroll who could be counted on to make bad impressions. One had a speech impediment, and another had two big moles on his face like that Motorhead guy who sang *Ace of Spades.* If you used him, you had to make sure he was angled to the camera so those moles were on full display.

Tab still worried, not only because Robert had gone pretty far this time, but also because he had to worry enough for the both of them. Robert lived on the surface, either because he didn't want to plumb the depths or because there were none to go spelunking within. He listened to Tab, but less and less as time went on.

"So now you agree this was a good move?" Robert asked.

"We're managing it well. Ratings were back up yesterday," Tab said.

"Back up to last year's peak?"

"Getting there."

"But we aren't there yet?"

"Soon."

"So we still aren't there?"

"Not as such."

"Godammit, give it to me straight."

"No."

Robert pushed back into the lumbar support of his office chair. He clasped his hands behind his head and breathed heavily. Then he rubbed his eyes.

"Look, Robert," Tab said. "All the signs are good. You took a huge risk, and it seems like it's paid off. Let's just get back to talking about how the Australians are to blame for problems in the Mideast, or something like that."

"You don't want me to mention Brewster again?"

"Why? There's no way to get more bang for the buck than we already have."

"And this other thing?"

"Harrogate? Look, the Brewster story was a one-hit wonder. It had shock value, but you know you'll just bore people if you do the same thing again with Cosmo.

Mention it, sure. But be quick about it. The first time was the charm. The second would be a rerun."

"All right, all right. I won't do the same story again."

"Please."

"Give me a break. I'm the one that takes these chances."

"And I'm the one who has to clean them up."

"But it's my ass out there. No one even knows who you are. Sometimes I don't anymore."

"Whatever."

Tab stood up without smiling. Even when he slouched, he still stood tall. But he was tired. And his wife had recently noticed a new wrinkle on his forehead. The Robert Lynch crevasse. Without smiling, that's what she named it.

Robert didn't smile either. Squinting his eyes, he scanned the bullet points that his staff prepared for that afternoon's program. News of the day. Updates on old stories. A few biographical notes to accompany file footage. He had to rub that page after mayo from his sandwich fell onto it. It left a grease stain, but he could still make out the words he didn't plan to read.

When Robert got onto the set, an assistant poked another sheet of paper at him. It revealed that the very same gun killed Jameson and Harrogate.

"You given this to Tab yet?"

"Nope," the assistant said. "Sorry about that."

"No, no. That's fine. He's got a headache. Uhh, just bury it in his inbox. Don't bother him with it."

The assistant started to say something, but Robert rudely trampled on his words with a deep, imperious tone.

"I have spoken."

When Robert heard the announcer say the program's title, he was ready. He'd keep his promise. He wouldn't reuse the Brewster routine on the Cosmo story. He'd try something different.

"In other news," Robert said near the end of his program. He liked using that transition. It made him feel like a journalist. "Cosmo Harrogate was found murdered yesterday. Now, I am sure all of you can imagine how I felt about him while he was alive. This man single-handedly raised millions for socialist causes and candidates. I'll wager that most Americans don't even know who he is. Unlike Brewster Jameson, the show-off, media whore that he was, Cosmo Harrogate was one of those backroom types who pull the very strings that have bound us into our leftwing nightmare."

At that moment, Robert deliberately paused, opening his ever-present bottle of water. Most of the anchors had coffee mugs on their news desks, but Robert had a bottle of water. He got money for product placement that way. Early in the show's success, he learned to use it as a prop. Opening it could create a good pause. Squeezing it inwards made a dramatic crackling sound. But Robert learned the hard way that he could only sip from it. He had guzzled water on that episode when he claimed the Masons were behind an international money-laundering scheme. He was actually thirsty, but the water went the wrong way and came out of his nose. It wasn't good TV.

Sip. Just sip.

"Now, I cannot say Cosmo was as dangerous as Brewster Jameson. Maybe he was. Maybe he was. All of you watching will have to make up your minds on that one, because I always want everyone to think on their own, for themselves, and come to their own conclusions. I said what I had to say about Jameson, and now I'm simply reporting the news of Harrogate's death. But, please, indulge me. Walk with me. Follow me."

Robert stood and began strolling around the set. He stopped and made a dramatic turn of the head. He tilted it downward a bit as he drew a breath and raised a finger to his lips. It made him look like he was thinking. After a couple of seconds, when it felt right, he lowered his hand and exhaled.

"The truth is, America, our friends in the police force have done their job, and, as always, they've done it well. We have just learned that the gun was used to shoot Cosmo Harrogate was the exact same gun that was used to shoot Brewster Jameson. It is safe to assume, therefore, that the very same person assassinated both men."

He looked upwards for a moment. That made him appear contemplative. Then he turned his head to another camera and took a deep breath.

"Now, I want to say something to our assassin. Excuse me, to our *hero.* I want to speak, now, directly to the man who is responsible for these two events. You see, I can't call these acts crimes because I am simply not sure that they are crimes. Everyone will have to think about that and come to their own decision, because I'm not sure."

Robert swallowed hard and then pursed his lips before licking them.

"What I want to say to the person responsible is this: Thomas Jefferson once told us that the tree of liberty must be refreshed from time to time with the blood of patriots and tyrants. Now, as all of you know, I'm a religious man, and as a result I remember that the Bible tells us an eye for an eye. I don't condone murder, but I strongly condone refreshing the tree of liberty. It would be unpatriotic to feel otherwise, wouldn't it, America?"

He breathed heavily as he walked back to his desk and sat down. He quietly kicked off his shoes.

"The socialists asked us to give peace a chance, but Thomas Jefferson asked us to do something else. Again, so I'm not misquoted by the liberal media, let me reiterate that I absolutely do not condone murder."

Brief pause.

"But I do condemn acts of treason."

Robert raised his right hand beside his head. His index finger pointed upwards, shaking just enough to underscore his next comment.

"Treason like the horrible events that are about to happen next week in New Orleans. *PushAhead.com,* a liberal think tank, will be holding their annual gathering. A meeting of minds. Dangerous minds. They're more dangerous than any assassin. They are holding our country hostage, and we have no choice but to target them and refresh the tree of liberty, at whatever the cost. Wise Up, America!"

The show ended, and the set went dark.

CHAPTER 8

Play Ball

By nature, I am a sociable guy, but I've never been particularly interested in exercise. During my twenties, I was active enough to keep trim. But somewhere around 33, it was as if everything went to hell. When I was young, I could hardly gain weight; now I have a gut that sticks out over my jeans. I used to be able to eat the spiciest foods; now I bloat like some damn puffer fish.

After the whole Cosmo mess, I needed to get out of the house, but how could a body not stay glued to the TV in the hours and days after big news events like bombings or hurricanes? Flipping channels between three or four news stations helped. Of course, you couldn't really do that during the commercials because they had colluded to take their station breaks in sync with one another.

So I flipped mid-sentence from one channel's anchor to the next. Sometimes it was as if the second one completed the first one's thought. Other times they were on very different wavelengths. Now, if they were all filming on location, you could occasionally glimpse the folks from one station in the background of the long shots of another. Funny.

I was stunned by how much time that all these folks were spending on Brewster and Cosmo. I had decided to think of them that way: Brewster and Cosmo, instead of Jameson and Harrogate. Last names are too impersonal. Not that I'd ever met Brewster, and my contact with

Cosmo was admittedly brief, but I still felt like I'd come to know them. Maybe it was because of all the biographical retrospectives on TV.

The fact that the media knew the same person killed both men was perfect. And I felt like Robert Lynch was speaking directly to me. Not in that crazy kind of way where a nut thinks that the dog next door is talking to him. Let's be clear about this. I'm certainly not nuts. I see a psychiatrist occasionally, and I do take my fair share of Prozac, but I am definitely not insane. No, it really seemed like Robert was encouraging me to keep going. That helped. Everyone needs a bit of encouragement. A pat on the back. Some acknowledgment that all the hard work and effort is worthwhile.

That was particularly important since I still needed to murder Numero Tres. My third victim, or at least my third victim in this series. It meant using the Glock, which was not a bad thing maybe. Not particularly interesting or new, but that was the point. Here directly, they would know the same person had chalked up a trio.

On TV, a professor of something-or-other claimed that the assassin was preaching to the public through his choice of gunshot wounds. The talking head didn't have a beard, and he wasn't that old, but he was a professor all the same, apparently.

"It's written in the bodies," he said. "You see, he's attacked the right side of the brain. This killer is no engineer. He is not a mathematician. No, no. He is in fact a thinker. An artist, if you will excuse the obvious insensitivity to the victims."

"But professor," the interviewer interjected. "You actually believe that the assassin has thought all of this through?"

"Undoubtedly."

To be honest, I hadn't realized that I had shot the right sides of their brains. To the best of my recollection, I had shot the left side of their heads. You see, from the side, well, the back-of-the-side, it *was* to the left. It was only the right side if you viewed the brains from the fronts of their heads.

That's where descriptions of automobiles are more understandable. Driver's side and passenger side are perfectly clear. Unless you were in England, but hell, I knew I'd never go to England. Jersey was as far east as I had ever gone, and that was far enough.

People's heads are a lot easier to shoot than understand.

Anyhow, I'll admit that I wasn't as ready for the spotlight as I had first believed. Funny thing, really. You want to get famous and you think about it often, but all that's bound up in wanting to be liked by lots of people, or in becoming rich. Stuff like that. The reality of fame is tough.

I confessed my fears to Frog, but as usual the pet rock was stone cold silent. Comforting, but quiet. So I phoned Chet.

We have quite a bit in common. Well, a little bit in common. In college, both of us drove old El Caminos. So badass. A truck and car, all in one. But that wasn't really true. It was half-truck and half-car, neither one thing nor the other. Real Twilight Zone stuff. Chet sold his El Camino sometime during law school. I kept mine, but it breaks down so often that most of the time it lives in my garage.

Chet was a smart guy, no doubt about it. Maybe it was because he had kids, and so he has to pretend to be a grown-up all the time, whereas single guys like me only have to put on that act for a few hours here and there.

It was a pleasant, sunny morning, but for some reason there weren't many people on the golf course. Perfect.

Both of us wore untucked Hawaiian shirts, a testament to our shared stomach expansions. At least he had the advantage of height, which helped conceal his gut to a degree.

Chet always had money enough for a golf cart and a caddy. He was a successful guy. He had a career. He was an *Er*. In his case it was a lawy*Er,* rather than a teach*Er* or a doct*Or.* And that bought something that money couldn't. It bought respect.

Our caddy kept his mouth shut, but he was breathing like he had a terrible cold or something. He coughed too, making a sound like his throat was full of phlegm soup. So I waited patiently until the third hole to pop the big question.

Chet sighed. "I just don't know how I'd handle fame. I guess it would be sweet to get interviewed on TV and stuff. Maybe sign autographs, too, huh?"

"So you've thought about it?"

"Sure. Hasn't everyone?"

"Well, what if you became famous for something different than what you wanted?"

"I don't get it. You mean like winning the lottery or surviving a plane wreck or something?"

"Yeah. Well, no. No, more like, say you wanted to be a judge famous for important rulings and writing books, but instead you became famous because someone in your courtroom was famous. Kind of a knock-on effect."

"Oh."

The caddy hacked up a glob that smeared some nearby blades of grass, so I dropped the subject until we made our way to the sixth hole.

"What if you knew that you could accidentally become famous, like in advance?"

"Don't follow you."

"Like say you were a judge and you knew you could recuse yourself from a case. Call in sick or something. But it was like a famous defendant, and you saw an opportunity to become Judge Ito or somebody."

"Well, Birch, you know, in high school, I wanted to be a jazz musician, and as a jazz musician, you have to improvise."

"I don't get it."

"Think of it like golf."

"Teed off?" I laughed uncomfortably.

The caddy gagged a bit, though it was unrelated to my joke. There was a frog in his throat, and it was no pet rock.

"No, like the rule book says."

"What have rules got to do with improvising?"

"Play the ball as it lies, play the course as you find it, and if you cannot do either, do what is fair."

That's why I dug Chet. He was confident in what he thought and said. He was a grown-up. He was an *Er*.

And his advice was to stay in the game. Go for the gold.

"You're three strokes over," Chet told me.

Triple bogey. Hot damn. The back of my neck ran with sweat. The caddy coughed up a yellow mass, which indicated that it was fairly well time to hit the clubhouse.

CHAPTER 9

Big and Easy

I hate dilettantes. When I do something, I try to do it as thoroughly and completely as possible. I have always tried so hard to know everything about the stuff that matters, and to ignore all the rest. The human brain can only hold so much, so I want to organize mine just right.

My iPod is loaded with every Cocker album I could find. Same goes for Asia. It was all there, even some bootleg live stuff. Asia was badass, even though they weren't really Asians. It was like they were foreign, but not that foreign.

I also have several classical mp3s, mainly Kathleen Battle doing Italian opera stuff. But those selections were just highlights, not the whole operas, which I definitely do not want to hear. So I renamed all of them on my computer. That way, if I die in a car wreck and someone goes through my things, they wouldn't spot the opera highlights. Can't have them thinking that I'm lowbrow.

Now, if someone was to ask me about Think Tanks, I could damn sure tell them a thing or two. Over the course of a few days, I devoured all the key stuff online. Not just the Wikipedia entry, but also the links to all the sources it used, and tons of other stuff I found on my own, including real books printed on real paper. I wanted to understand the background, and to smell the knowledge for myself, right off the ink.

Traveling to New Orleans, I kept worrying that the whole thing might be a bum steer, or even a set up. There was no way to misinterpret Robert's directive about PushForward. At least three hundred people would be at their confab, and I selected my prey from among them, as well as a having a couple of backup targets ready in case of cancellations.

For the first time, it occurred to me how similar the words "prey" and "pray" are. Like as not, that's no mistake.

Clearly PushForward would have security. That would be standard. But would they be expecting an assassin thanks to Robert's broadcast? One has to be cagey. That's why I brought some French Quarter maps. Studying those helped me to learn all the back alleys and escape routes.

And if you get cornered, be selfish. Use one bullet on yourself. Position the gun barrel at the back-of-the-side of your own head. Go out like the others. If possible, see that Frog makes a clean getaway. Throw him to safety. Rock on, pal.

Approaching New Orleans, I was struck by how amazingly different it was from Oklahoma City. Both places are hot and humid, but there was something about the trees and swamps and everything else in Louisiana. It was different. I couldn't quite put my finger on it, so I decided to concentrate on something else.

The French Quarter was always popular, but the fact that it was Vieux-to-Do meant that it was extra busy. One weekend and three festivals. It was a perfect time to get lost in the crowd. To go unnoticed. Blend in with the locals till you do the deed.

It wasn't hard to learn where Michael Gerber was staying. Tearing open a new cell phone and inserting the sim card, I waited in my hotel room. I bought the phone at a dollar store in Texas. It was a cheap, and it was perfect. Pay as you go.

So I did. Phoning all the top hotels in and around the Quarter didn't take long. I pretended that I was with the *New York Times,* you know, wanting to interview Gerber about the Nawlins confab. As it happened, Gerber had taste. He was staying at the Soniat House, which was made up of a few old townhouses not far from Jackson Square. Very nice. Good view from the balcony, probably. But too small to be a crime scene, at least for this big of a crime.

I scarfed down some jambalaya and Blackened Voodoo beer at the Gumbo Boy, then scouted out the Soniat. Gerber's talk would be over by now, and probably his dinner too. The trick would just be to wait and wait and, if need be, to wait some more.

Gerber was a U.S. representative from Wisconsin. That's right. Or, no, maybe it was Vermont. I justified my inability to remember by the fact I had spent most of my time studying the history of Think Tanks. Anyways, Gerber was pretty far out there politically, at least according to WNB. In some old broadcasts, Robert had dubbed him "Lefty."

A nickname like that made Gerber sound mobbed up. Too bad he wasn't Italian, you know, with a name like "Giovanni" or something. Lefty Giovanni. Now that's a mobster's name. Lefty Gerber wasn't fit for a Scorsese movie, but it got the point across. According to one WNB study, he was the most liberal politician in Congress.

I was shocked to see what looked to be Gerber and some cute young gal emerge from the Soniat onto Chartres Street. What the hell? Gerber's talk was at the Convention Center, so he should've been out, not in. But it was him, all the same. Same face, same hair, same big-and-tall body, and the same eyes, which made him look as if he was always sleepy, like he had just gotten out of bed.

He and the chick turned down a narrow passage at the side of the hotel, so everything looked right. Crowds nearby. So many of them, whooping and hollering, and all that loud music going. It would muffle any scream. No one else appeared to be down that little street, so, without even bothering to turn off my iPod, I spoke.

"Excuse me, sir, but can I get your autograph?"

Gerber must have immediately spied the gun badly hidden under my leather jacket. He turned away quick, but not so fast that I couldn't see the glint of fear in his eyes, which all of a sudden looked wide awake. And he darted from the scene but quick, leaving his gal flat.

I took off after him, without even bothering to remove my ear buds. The gal followed. Not good. Not good at all. Big Easy, my ass.

Gerber nearly collided with a chunky jazz clarinet-tist playing on the street, but in trying to miss her, he smashed into the cart that held her compact discs. They must not have been shrink wrapped, because soon it began to rain CDs and jewel cases.

In an effort to be polite and not to trample on top of them, I tacked to the right, accidentally knocking over what was either a short clown or a kid holding cotton candy. Not cool. And not invisible. Plus I swallowed the butterscotch in my mouth.

At least Gerber was kind enough to zoom behind a church. I looked around to see if anyone was watching, but the coast was clear. That's when I pulled the trigger. Silencers are golden, and bullets are platinum. Gerber's body seemed to flail midair at a 45-degree angle before landing on the ground, the bullet hitting him in his leg or ass maybe. Asia's *Cutting It Fine* provided the background music while I loomed over him. Their music sounds better on the original LP, but I couldn't do anything about that under the conditions that prevailed.

"No, please," Gerber cried, "Don't. Look, no one heard. You can just stop. Please, stop."

"Look away," I demanded.

Gerber turned, exposing the wrong side of his head.

"Look the other way."

Gerber reluctantly turned his head the other direction, and there it was. The spot. The holy of holies. The back-of-the-side-of-the-head. So I squeezed the trigger. His blood Jackson Pollocked all over the sidewalk.

Thanks to the silencer, nobody heard squat. But at least one person saw what went down. Gerber's gal. She'd been chasing after us and arrived just in time to witness the money shot.

For the first time, I got a good look at her. She had bobbed black hair. Maybe there was a hint of dark purple to it, but with the sun going down it was hard to tell. Glitter was the main ingredient of her eye shadow, and she had on more makeup than she did clothes. Her small chest heaved in and out because she was out of breath. I declare, she was hot as a firecracker.

"Are you him?," she asked in between huffs and puffs. "The assassin?" She was smiling. One side of her face looked shy, and the other seductive.

"Who wants to know?"

God, I said that awkwardly, but I had no script on which to rely.

"I'm Sadie." She flashed her smile again. "They say you're a folk hero."

"What about what's-his-name on the ground?"

"What about him?"

Sadie was not stable. A dog walking could see that. She broke a heel during the chase, so she had to keep tiptoeing one foot in a feeble effort to stay level.

"Come here," Sadie said as she trundled through her purse. She took my arm, forcefully pushed my jacket and shirtsleeve upwards, and then used her eyeliner to write a series of numbers on my forearm. Her handwriting wasn't great, but in fairness, my skin wasn't resting on a flat surface.

"Call me."

There wasn't any "Please" or "If You Want To." Just two words and a crooked smile that looked as much like a command as an invitation. My tum-tum churned, but it could have just been the jambalaya.

Big Easy, my ass, I thought again, but this time in a different mental tone of voice.

CHAPTER 10

Air Time

"I imagine you know what they're calling you?" Big Jim Toll asked me sarcastically.

Toll wasn't the top-rated jock at Oklahoma radio station KCOM, but he was good at what he did, and far better at it than anyone else on the air in the middle of the night. I had never met him but sometimes tuned into his program when I couldn't sleep. Radio was still king. Well, no, it wasn't, but I liked to pretend that it was.

Everyone else in the media was talking about Gerber and the others, so why shouldn't I? It wasn't like I was just in it for the money. That's why I called Big Jim's hotline and set up the freebie interview. Time to mold the media coverage. To press the press, so to speak.

I spent all day practicing answers to likely questions into a wooden spoon while Frog played audience. If only I had one of the old, 1940s-style microphones. 'Course by the time the show started, I didn't need either. Just another throwaway cell phone. A fella can't take too many chances these days.

Part of the plan was to make Big Jim understand. And for Big Jim to like me. I liked Big Jim, so I hoped for a little of the same in return. He didn't seem like the kind of guy who'd say "Aw Shucks."

"Sure, I know they've given me a name. I had no choice in the matter, but that's how it goes," I replied in a chipper voice. "Makes no nevermind to me."

"The Artist," Big Jim said. "That's the name."

"Well, I guess that comes from the whole back-of-the-side-of-the-head thing."

"You mean you've assassinated three people by firing bullets into their right brain?"

"Yeah. Well, the last part is true."

"So you mean to tell all the good folks in our listening audience that you *didn't* shoot Brewster Jameson, Cosmo Harrogate, and Representative Gerber?"

"I killed them. All three of them. That's the point. I can see that any one of them on its own might be considered an assassination, but together they really add up to something different."

"I don't understand."

"Think about Lee Harvey Oswald. He tried to shoot General Walker, but failed."

"Then he shot JFK."

"Well, there's some dispute about that. He was a patsy."

"So I've heard."

"My point is, even if Oswald did shoot Kennedy, and I'm not saying he did, that's just one. Not two, and certainly not three."

"I don't get it."

"Well, there's a great deal of difference between an assassin and a serial killer."

"You think of yourself as a serial killer?"

"Don't you?"

"I suppose so. I think we've all been focussing on the fact these three people were political figures. All three were unpopular with many Americans, at least those who knew who they are."

"Who they *were.*"

"Huh?"

"Past tense. No big deal."

"Let me put it to you this way. The mainstream media believes these murders were politically motivated. That you chose them for that reason. Ergo, you assassinated them."

I didn't respond. I hadn't talked into the spoon about that.

"Well, let's go back to this whole Artist angle. Do you think it fits?"

"I don't know that I consider myself to be an Artist, but I'll be happy to answer to that name if you want."

"We can use your real name if you prefer."

"Uhh, that'd be a big no."

"Moving on. How did you come to want to destroy the right brain, especially when you're assassinating lefties? Do you hate math?"

"No, I don't hate math."

"Were you trained in art?"

"I had art classes."

"In college?"

"Grammar school."

"Did you get good grades?"

"My pictures of the grassy knoll used a lot of good perspective. That's what my teacher said."

"We're going to have to leave it there for a few minutes for the news and some important words from the good folks who pay to keep this place open."

Big Jim put me on hold for awhile, and then picked up the phone again. This time he sounded different. Quite a bit lighter. It was his real voice.

"Okay then."

"Are we back on the air?"

"Not yet. Color radar weather is still ahead."

"You aren't turning me in, are you? Or tracing this call?"

"Hell, no. Everyone in the country hated those bastards you killed. You did shoot them, right? KCOM don't need no more damn scandals."

"Would that include interviewing a serial killer?"

"No. I mean, are you really who you say you are?"

"You mean, am I a fake?"

"Yes, sir. A phony or something?"

"No, I'm not a fake. I'm the real deal."

"So you *are* the Artist."

"Sure."

"For real?"

"As sure as the sun will cross the sky."

"Well, okay then."

"And I've got deep convictions about these things."

"Whoa. Whoa. Hold on!"

Big Jim changed his voice again. It got deeper as he sent it down the elevator shaft of his throat.

"And we are back, people. We are back with the exclusive, first-ever interview with the man with the plan. The man that I personally would call the Exterminator, but that wouldn't be fair to him, because that would probably say more about his victims than him. So we'll keep using the moniker that the big boys in the media gave him this past week. He's the Artist. And the Artist has got a lot to say. Paint a picture for everyone out in radio land."

Pause.

More pause. I remained silent.

"Yeah, so with that in mind, let's get back to the questions."

The second half of the interview was basically uneventful, until Big Jim read from an online dictionary.

"I don't know if it's worth arguing the point," he said, right before proceeding to argue the point. "It says here on the computer that an assassin is a murderer, particularly in cases of killing a prominent person for fanatical or monetary reasons. Now you said you weren't an assassin, but this sounds like you."

Pause.

"Did you take money to off these three guys?"

More pause.

"Did you have fanatical reasons?"

Even more pause.

"You got any response to that, Artist? Come on, now. We're talking about the big questions here. Life and death. Don't you have anything to say?"

"Read off the first three letters of the word assassin. That's my response."

I hung up, left my house, and drove around for an hour or two until I was sure no one was following me. Behind a vacant grocery store, I put the truck in park, left it running, got out, and sledgehammered my latest cell phone into five or ten pieces before chunking it into the trash.

On the way back home, I rolled down the driver's window. The cold air outside felt better than the hot air inside.

CHAPTER 11

Sadie May

I hate tardiness. To me, it's one of the main reasons why people fail in this life. You've got to be on time. Showing up is half the battle. That's why I drove to St. Louis one day early, checked into a decent hotel, and then located the restaurant over an hour before I needed to be there.

Sadie lived in Chicago, and so we'd agreed to meet somewhere in between. When she spoke on the phone, she had this silky voice, almost like some old torch singer. Very breathy. She should really have been on the radio. I hadn't noticed it so much when we met in New Orleans, but in fairness, we were kind of rushed that day.

It was about nine months earlier that I had broken up with Ginny. She was attractive, with long brown hair, and she was nice. Goodhearted and all that. She was one of those gals whose teeth were too big for her mouth, and when she grinned, you'd see a lot of gum.

But Ginny's sister had gotten knocked up out of wedlock, and after that Ginny just seemed distant. All of the hotness simmered before cooling down completely. Funny, but I can't remember her phone number anymore, even though I can recall a few other old numbers, including one for a chick I didn't like. I did write Ginny a great poem, lots of verses and rhymes, but that was after we parted ways, so I was the only person who read it.

Serial monogamy treated me well over the years. Ginny was the latest in year after year of romances.

Thinking back, none of my girlfriends seemed to have much in common with each other. Despite all of her big teeth, Ginny was quiet, but some of the others were loud. A few were preppy, but one had been an out-and-out hippy, totally granola.

Another had really tried to do a number on me. She fixed me a BLT once that had some bits of broken glass in it. No one believed me later, but that's the gospel truth. In between the tomatoes were tiny shards of glass. When I confronted her, she claimed it was an accident, that she had broken some dish earlier in the day. But I reckon that deep down she must have wanted to be a serial killer too.

'Course women that don't feed you glass can be awful clingy. They don't get that a fella has to devote a lot of time to his work in order to get ahead in this world. I hoped that Sadie would understand that, and that she would turn out to be even-tempered and level-headed. After all, she had been dating a Congressman.

I knew that Miceli's was expensive. I had seen *$$$* next to its name in a restaurant guide, and this came during a month that had already cost me plenty. Hotels, fuel, and food. That's why I knew not to flinch when I got the bill. I didn't want to look cheap, not in front of Sadie, not at first at least.

After wasting time in every store near the restaurant, I finally decided to waltz into the foyer a couple of minutes after the hour. I wanted to appear fashionably late. But Sadie was nowhere in sight, so that plan went all to hell. She wouldn't know whether I was two minutes late or two hours early.

A waiter seated me at a table for two. He promised he'd bring menus, but then he off and disappeared. See, that's another problem with the modern world. No dedication. No follow through. So I had sit there with nothing to do, not with my hands or anything. And I stifled the urge to suck on a butterscotch, fearing my breath would smell like somebody's grandmother. Welcome to Schmoeland.

"Do you just go by The Artist now, or can I call you Birch?"

Sadie tittered after she said that. She had sneaked up behind me and leaned down to speak. At last.

"C'mon, don't embarrass me now. I didn't…"

"No, of course you didn't think up that crazy name. And don't worry, no one here knows us, silly billy."

She cooed. She really cooed when she spoke. It was like listening to chocolate melt slowly.

The waiter interrupted us with the long-lost menus, which caused Sadie to get even perkier. She made a low, guttural sound, like she was sexually excited by food. Then she moistened her lips with the tip of her pink tongue.

"I'm so starved. God, I can really eat." Then came another one of those low, cavernous sounds.

Sadie knew what she was doing. Starter, then a pasta dish, and then meat. It was the full-on Italian meal, complete with the biggest steak the restaurant had on offer.

She was so damned ravenous, it was like she hadn't eaten all day. In fairness, she had flown from Chicago to St. Louis. Airplane meals are awful, and airport food isn't much better. She might have fasted. Or maybe she just had an out-of-whack metabolism thing going on.

"BRB, Baby. Powder time."

Sadie disappeared, but not so fast that I couldn't stare at her prancing to the restroom. She was thinner than I remembered. Her butt was so small that it didn't shake when she walked.

She was back in a flash, like she either had superpowers or she didn't really have to go after all. Or maybe she had a small bladder, like that British whats-his-name.

"So, what did I miss?" Then she snorted a bit, almost to prevent me from answering.

For the first time my eyes locked on her most distinctive feature. Sadie's cheeks kind of pushed out. Yeah, she had beautiful eyes that looked like pools of blah, blah, blah, and pretty skin and all that. Nice short hair. Her makeup was sexy. She had some kind of turquoise eye stuff on, bright lipstick, and glitter. Glitter everywhere. "Sadie dust," she called it, when she noticed me noticing her. Then she scrunched her nose a bit, like she was using it to push up non-existent glasses.

But those cheekbones. It was like she was a little chipmunk, a hot-as-hell little chipmunk, but I knew that I had to keep my mouth shut about that, never mentioning it, even if we became an item. Not even if we got married. Because she wouldn't understand that it was a compliment. The chipmunk thing is a great look.

That was when I decided to use my old strategy. Don't talk about yourself. Don't bring up Lee Harvey Oswald or Asia. And don't talk about pet rocks. Just ask questions about Her. And none that are very specific. Give her wide berth.

Somehow she stuffed her face while simultaneously offering her dime store biography, but none of it seemed rude or gross. It was stimulating. And when she went after her steak with that ridged knife, it was sexy, more than anything she said. I felt a lump in my pocket, and it damn sure wasn't Frog.

Sadie May Johnson was born in Arkansas, but moved to Chicago after getting her college degree in Little Rock. She was 28. So young. She was a writer, but hadn't written anything yet. There had been a few boyfriends, but nothing serious. Michael Gerber was nice, and yeah, they had slept together, but it didn't mean much. He was single, and so he frequented the Adult Friend-type sites without fear of scandals, except that he did use a fake name and wore a half-mask in his online photo.

Then Sadie said that New Orleans was a blast until Gerber died, not that she held that against me. She worked at a travel agency in Chicago, putting in so many hours that she never got to go anywhere herself. First Cajun country; now St. Louis. Her first two trips outside of the move to Illinois. No, she didn't have a passport. Someday, though. Someday she would really go places.

Sadie forked the last few bites of steak off my plate after devouring her own. No shame. Just matter of fact. The waiter was unimpressed, but she didn't seem to care. After his initial absence, the bastard had taken to hovering.

"Ice cream time. Two scoops of vanilla for me."

I wasn't surprised that she could still eat, but would never have pegged her as vanilla. I just sat and watched her gum it down, which didn't take long. Her spoonfuls were enormous, and somehow she avoided brain freeze. Gal's got talent, I thought.

A tiny bit of her dessert fell off the spoon and onto her chest, but I steadfastly refused to look. I wanted to, but I figured I'd get caught, and, well, I didn't want to seem solely focused on sex. She was so intent on eating that she didn't seem to notice anything.

Her spoon clanked into the empty dessert glass, and then came another one of those guttural sounds. "Done now!"

And so we left, me bumping into the waiter on the way out the door.

After walking up to a stoplight, Sadie turned her head towards a shopping mall. The wind blew her little dress, and I saw right down it. No bra, and tiny tits with big, hard nipples.

When she turned towards me, Sadie grinned as if she hadn't a care in the world, then she reached over and kissed me on the lips. It lasted a long time, but there were no tongues, or even that kind of movement of the heads from 10 o'clock to 2 o'clock or even 11 to 1. Instead, it was like she was kissing me head-on, finally releasing my face by placing her hands on my cheeks and ending with an intentionally loud smack sound.

As we resumed our walk, Sadie grilled me. She did it with a smile, but she grilled me all the same. Her cooing voice disappeared, replaced with the clipped sharpness of a cross-examination. And each new question came the very instant after I finished the previous answer. It was like she had all of it planned out in advance.

I didn't mind. Some of it was tit-for-tat. Basic biography and wish list stuff. Some of it was about serial killing, but those questions weren't any harsher in tone than the others. And I have to say that I felt good about my answers. I had already rehearsed most of them into my wooden spoon.

When we got in line at the movie theatre, she resumed her cooing, breathing out vague compliments about my "career" and how I was really going places.

So I decided to her ask her back to my hotel room. I was thinking about her flat chest when the guy at the box-office said $18. And that's when the whole evening transformed into disaster.

My wallet was missing.

Was it at the restaurant? Had I been pickpocketed? My forehead felt numb, and my armpits began to sweat. Without those credit cards, I was screwed.

"We'd better go back," I told her. "Maybe I left it at Miceli's."

"I think I'm in love with you, Baby, but I'm heading to my hotel now. Call me in a couple-uhh-three days when I'm back in Chicago." Sadie looked deep into my eyes, let out another guttural sound, and then walked off. After several steps, she turned back to check if I was still watching her. Seeing that I was, she smiled widely and cocked her head to the side a bit, then turned back around and began walking again.

I frantically retraced my steps. My walk turned into a sprint. I wanted to think about what was right with Sadie, and what was wrong with Sadie. But wallet panic took up all the real estate in my head.

After reaching Miceli's, I stepped inside, out of breath. The host said someone would be with me shortly.

CHAPTER 12

Bushwhacked

"Dumbass says What."

That's a terrible thing to do to somebody during a conversation. The other person is thrown by it, especially if it's been muttered under the breath, and so they say "what" in response. God, some people can be so rude. And I revile folks who are rude.

Something similar happens when a person calls out your name. Somebody yells "John" in a crowded store, and every damned John in the place turns around. Force of habit. Maybe it's some kind of innate identification each person has with their own name, hearing it over and over again, for years and years since they were a little kid.

"Hey! Artist!"

That's what the guy yelled, and, sure enough, I whizzed around without thinking twice. Funny how quick you can get used to a new name.

And things were going so well. My wallet was history, but Chet had wired enough money to get me home. Replacement credit cards arrived in short order. And I got another stab at my driver's license photo. No biggie.

After leaving her a couple of messages, Sadie finally called me back. She was so sexy over the phone, joyfully recalling the steak she had eaten and the movie that had got away. It probably wasn't any good, she said without a trace of regret.

I was leaving a bookstore when she phoned, and so I stopped right outside the front door. She was commanding all of my attention up until I heard the Artist remark. Then the same voice shouted again.

"It's him! Quick!"

A guy in his mid-twenties ran towards me, accompanied by a hefty thug brandishing a video camera. The red light was on.

"There you are!" the guy screamed.

"I'm sorry. I don't understand," I replied, attempting to regain my composure. My tongue shifted a butterscotch around inside my mouth. "Could you please shut that camera off?"

"Well, I don't know. Can you shut your phone off?"

The guy had one of those smirk faces, like he knew he was arrogant and was proud of it. He smiled, but even when he stopped smiling, the smirk was still there.

I spoke to Sadie, getting off the phone by telling her there was some unexpected trouble.

"So it is you!"

"Huh?" I responded, trying to appear clueless.

"Get a tight closeup," the smirk guy told the camera thug, before clearing his throat and turning back to me. "Can you tell us how you first got started?"

"Started?"

"Assassinating political figures in these United States."

"You guys cops?"

My butterscotch came unstuck from one tooth and clanked against another.

"No, are you?"

"Huh?"

"We're journalists."

"What station?"

"Do you kill because you want to, or because you have to?"

I had seen this before. WNB did it all the time. Surprise folks on the street when you can't schedule a proper interview with them. I felt the impulse to flee, but my limbs seemed to be frozen.

There was a long pause after Smirk's question. I didn't say anything.

"Mr. Dictionary run away on you? I asked you why you kill people."

"Hold your horses. I don't know who you people are, but you've got the wrong guy."

I said those words in as calm a tone of voice as I could muster, knowing that damned red light on the camera was still burning as bright as the fires of hell. Then I just up and stormed off.

The less-than-dynamic duo followed, with Smirk flanking my left and Thug my right. Those boys had gumption.

"Look, we'll shut off the camera for a minute if you just hold up," Smirk claimed.

I stopped dead in my tracks, turned around, and stared while the red light dimmed.

"You *are* him, aren't you? We've been following you all morning. We know where your house is. We know everything."

"Who are you people?"

Without intending to do it, my tongue elevated the butterscotch between my upper teeth and cheek. It poked out like a bit of chewing tobacco.

"We're freelancers," Smirk said. "I'm Andrew White, and we're the Ambushers."

"That's what they call us," Thug added, speaking for the first time, still out of breath from hustling it.

"Where from?"

"Washington."

"State?"

"No, D.C."

"God, you must have spent a lot on gas to get all the way to Oklahoma."

"We flew. Now, let's talk about assassinations."

"Why are you doing this to me?"

"An anonymous informant tipped us off."

"Jim Fat Ass Toll?"

"No."

"I'm just a patsy."

"We don't want to arrest you. We just want to talk."

"I don't cash checks for strangers."

"Come on, dude. Really, we just want to talk."

"Off the record?"

"Well, the camera's off."

"So how did you find me?"

"It was a tip from St. Louis."

I thought about my lost wallet, and all those things that Sadie said over dinner, about assassinations and other junk. The Jameson jig was up. The waiter had ratted me out.

"Really. We just want to talk," Smirk said. "About whatever you want."

I put my hands in my pockets. Frog was there, but he was too small to properly brain Smirk, let alone Thug. Maybe Frog could put out an eye, but then again, he was too precious to risk.

All the nearby streets were packed with cars, with plenty of folks rubbernecking us. Two or three even honked their horns at the sight of Thug's camera. Why do people do that? Honk when they see cameras? And it's always got to be two or three quick honks, rather than one long one. Like they've never seen a camera before.

"So you seemed unhappy with the radio interview?"

"Well, it's like this. I'm not an assassin."

"You want to be thought of as a serial killer?"

"Yeah, that's it. Basically."

"Basically?"

"I am a serial killer, except that I also find that term kind of problematic."

"How so?"

I turned my head and spit the remains of the butterscotch into a hankerchief, then stood up straight, the best I could.

"Well, if you stop and think about it, the term isn't very politically correct."

"What would you prefer to be called?"

At that point, I wished the red light was back on. I had given my answer to the wooden spoon so many times.

"The appropriate term, the one that is accurate and least offensive to those of us in this line of work, is Repeat Life Snuffer."

"Repeat Life Snuffer? That's what you want to be?"

"That's what I am."

It wasn't political correctness that caused me to say that, because I'm not P.C. Not at all, quite the opposite, really. But I want to hang my own hat on a new term, to get credited with inventing something. Maybe even get into *Bartlett's Quotations*. Then I launched into some of my other canned answers without even waiting for more questions. We must have talked for at least five minutes.

"And that's it for Andrew White and the Ambushers."

Smirk said that in the general direction of Thug, like he was on TV or something. Clearly something was wrong with him. And Thug, well, Thug was just sweating his big boy sweat.

"Thanks for the interview, pal."

"Whoa, there, fella. I need to know. Are you going to tell the cops about me?"

"We just wanted an interview. But you probably don't need to worry about cops."

"Huh?"

"You seen the polls lately? You're numbers are starting to get better than the President. You're popular."

I stared at him dumbly.

"Not George Clooney popular, but popular."

Then the Ambushers ambled away. It was a close one. But maybe no harm done. Later Smirk would probably mention something on the news about an off-the-record source. Truth be told, he was probably a better interviewer than Big Jim.

Sinking into my living room chair later in the day, I was happy enough. Frog was on the TV tray right beside my Peach Nehi. Time to relax.

After an hour of reading, I switched on the TV. It was going to provide background noise while I went to take a leak, but I stopped short when an WNB anchor said, "Repeat Life Snuffer."

There I was on TV, talking with Smirk, discussing killing and ballistics and all the jabber that I shared off-the-record. The image quality was poor, and kind of shaky. Vomit inducing, really. Thug must have had a hidden camera, like the news guys use when they do a sting operation on restaurants with filthy kitchens.

Worst of all, my name flashed on the screen. Birch, aka The Artist. The real question was whether or not the Ambushers would reveal my last name. Only time would tell, but I was too impatient to sit around waiting for the answer.

CHAPTER 13

Live from New York

It was 3:17 AM. All the good people were asleep. All the interesting people were awake. I didn't lay claim to either category, but I was up just the same. That meant Frog was up as well.

To be honest, both of us were scared of the police and scared of everyone and everything, so we tooled around town until we reached an old park, the one where the pushers push and the druggies drug. Wearing rubber gloves, I whipped out my 9mm, removed the clip, dry fired, separated the slide from the lower receiver, then took out the spring and barrel. Rubbed each piece carefully to remove fingerprints, and then restarted my truck. From there, we hit five dumpsters in five different locations, all of them located behind crummy old stores that didn't appear to have security cameras. Having reached my victim quota of three, it seemed best to get rid of the weapon, piece by piece. For self-defense reasons, I'd buy another right away, at a gun show of course. It'd have a clean history.

Me and Frog rushed home to honker down, even though I knew that home would be the first place that They would look for me. When I shoved a desk up to the front door, I thought of Smirk. When I jammed a wooden chair under the back doorknob, I thought of Smirk. And when I slammed my fist into a filing cabinet repeatedly, I thought of Smirk. Someday I'll be having that grin of his.

The papers inside the cabinet were in folders sus-
pended on little wire hooks. They held El Camino
schematics, except for the bottom drawer, which con-
tained old photocopies on Asia and some other eighties
rock bands. Each time my fist hit the cabinet, they
shook, and as they did, I imagined Smirk's internal
organs doing the same.

Over and over again, the news replayed clips from
Thug's hidden camera, each clearly edited out of con-
text to place me in the worst possible light. Fortunately,
the image quality was poor, so it was hard to make
out my face in any detail. That was also true of some
photos that caught me in long shots. At least two
showed me in the same location as the interview, but
from a different angle than the footage. Smirk and
Thug must have had a friend, some triangulated bastard hidden in a knoll.

Slumping uneasily into my easy chair, I closed my
eyes and thought about sounds. Not images, but sounds.
So many great sounds produced in this world are lost to
time. Still cameras used to make lots of noise, like when
you shut the camera door, or when the film rewound.
That's to say nothing of the sound of Polaroids spitting
out those funny smelling pictures.

Digital cameras had nothing on the old models. Sure,
they captured images, but that was about it. And those
images won't last, not like hard copies, or tintypes.

After a few minutes, more or less, I reopened my
eyes and stared. The entire house was dark, except for
the flicker from the TV.

The surprising part was that WNB anchors defended
my rights. They spoke about my right to bear arms. They
spoke about the evil of secular progressives. And they
read poll numbers from snap surveys.

The Artist had a thirty-eight percent favorable rating. Twenty-five percent disapproved of him. Seventeen percent said they had never heard of him. That left a lot of people unaccounted for. They must not have understood English, or not answered their phones when the pollsters called.

Finally a middle-of-the-night rebroadcast of *Wise Up, America!* came on. I figured that however Robert went, so went the nation. Or at least enough people to make a difference. My biggest fear was that Robert would experience a change of heart, maybe call me a wuss.

But that's not what happened. Robert praised me, over and over again. And so for the first time in several years, I actually felt proud. Sure, I was proud of my JFK assassination book collection, and I was proud of my El Camino, but this was about stuff that I'd accomplished, not just stuff that I owned. And, hell, it was right there on TV.

A lot of media types bashed Robert, but maybe the guy was okay. More than all okay, maybe. And he was kind of my new friend, in a way. That's certainly how it felt when the Voice phoned me from WNB early the next morning.

"Do I have to drive up there? I mean, that's a long way, and what with gas prices the way they are…"

"No, no," the Voice said. "We'll book your flight. First class tickets. And a room at the Waldorf Astoria."

"Do I get paid?"

"I'm afraid we can't pay you," the Voice explained with a well-rehearsed sound of regret. "You see, that would constitute a violation of our journalistic ethics."

"Oh, sure. I can understand that."

"You'll need to get packed quickly. We can get you on a flight this afternoon."

"Sure, sure. Now, what about the authorities or whatever?"

"No one knows your last name but a few of us, and we won't reveal it. We'd be violating our journalistic ethics to give up a source."

"What about Smirk and Thug?"

"Who?"

"The Ambushers."

"We purchased their footage and they had to sign a confidentiality agreement with us."

"Oh. Well, in that case…"

"Great! The hotel room will be in my assistant's name. We'll send a car for you tomorrow morning at 11 AM. That will give you plenty of time before Robert's show."

In the space of mere hours, I had gone from the fear of tossing salads to the thrill of Waldorf salads. I threw some wrinkled clothes into a satchel, knowing that a good hotel would have an ironing board, and headed to the airport. Better be at least two hours early, if not earlier.

While waiting to board, I rang Sadie. She cooed me onwards, saying it was the opportunity of a lifetime. Don't I know it. This was What It Was All About.

Arriving at WNB, I was impressed with how pleasant everyone was, especially given that it was New York, and I detest the very notion of New York. They gave me a quick tour before ushering me into makeup. An intern even asked for my autograph. I started to sign *Birch,* but quickly changed the B into a kind of screwed-up looking A, and then added the remaining letters of my new name. R-T-I-S-T. Afterwards, I backed the pen up to add the definitive article THE in front of it.

In the Green Room, the Voice became a Face. Tab something or other. Tab. Like the diet drink. Got it.

He was the producer, and his first words were pretty tough. No other program would give The Artist this chance, especially insulating him from the police. Be careful what you say, all that kind of thing. But then he finished real nice, full of "Thanks" and "Glad to Have Yous."

Right after *Wise Up, America!* started, Robert launched into his regular feature *Tort, Tort, and Retort.* It gave him a chance to rail against trial lawyers and judges and to pass judgment on them. Sometimes he beat up on juries too. Real equal opportunity stuff. Not at all fake news.

I was disappointed that a story about recent Supreme Court decision on imminent domain was more important than my TV debut, but Tab explained everything. A few advertisers were worried about Robert's coverage of The Artist, so there was no choice but to bury me in the middle of the show. That gave everyone a bit of cover.

When the time finally came, Robert sauntered around his set, a tear forming in his eye. He usually built up to the tear, but there it was, right from the start of the segment. And then he yammered all about American exceptionalism, and how few people really believe in that anymore, and how few people work hard to achieve The American Dream.

"Now America, I've told you The Artist is a real American hero." When he said that, the same words appeared on the bottom of the screen, just above the ticker tape news.

"And I've told you that he is a modern day Paul Revere, riding into our collective imagination with an important warning about all that is rotten in our country today. He's more than Paul Revere, really. He's like one of the four horsemen. And I'm not kidding here people. Several important thinkers have told me that, including the author of a series of novels about the Rapture. Now, I can't verify that he's really one of the horsemen, but…"

It was about that time that Robert's tear evaporated. After swallowing some spit, his voice grew louder and stronger.

"Wise Up, America! The Artist has said, 'Come and see,' and so I saw. We saw. And we've got to keep looking."

His lower teeth gently bit into his upper lip as his head shook up and down slightly. It was the build-up to something important.

"The Artist is a man, and he's more of a man than any politician, I can tell you that. And he's from Oklahoma. He's from Oklahoma, and he has emerged onto our national stage like a modern-day Horatio Alger, leaving his Fly Over State — and don't get me wrong, I love Fly Over States, Salt of the Earth, honest to God — and he left his Fly Over State to confront the problems we face head-on. And I'm very proud that he's my guest today."

Come time for me to enter from stage left, it felt like a long walk.

After sitting in a chair next to his desk, I tried to shake Robert's hand. It seemed to be the polite thing to do. After all, we hadn't met backstage. But Robert didn't take the bait, launching instead into a reserved smile and "Thank You for Being Here," yada yada yada.

For the first time, I noticed that Robert had a square jaw. My uncle once said that crazy people always have square jaws. That gal who fed me the glass sandwich had one.

Robert's questions came fast and furious. That's how he rolled.

"Who do you most admire, would you say?"

"The Zodiac, probably. He got to have it both ways. Fame and anonymity. That's rare, especially in today's world."

"But I'm sure you have other heroes?" Robert asked, clearly displeased with my answer.

"Oh yes. George Washington and Abraham Lincoln."

"Wonderful," Robert smiled. We were finally starting to hit it off.

"Now, some would call you a criminal, a murderer, an assassin. I'll admit you're a bit of a scofflaw, but I'd have to add that there are times when we have to break the rules. The founding fathers all had a bit of mischief in them. And, I mean, I'd run a red light if I had to get someone dying of a heart attack to the hospital, wouldn't you, America?"

On that last bit, Robert looked into a different camera. Then he turned back to me without saying anything. Another pause.

"How would you respond, Artist?"

"It's my belief that we don't own our own bodies. They are on loan from God."

Frog always liked that line. He'd watched me speak it into the wooden spoon twenty or thirty times. More maybe.

"And we're out, guys," the Voice said. Tab's voice boomed from parts unknown.

"Is this a commercial break?"

"No," Robert said. "NATO has started bombing some country in the Middle East. Looks like war, maybe. They've had to go to the live desk for action news."

"Action news? So...the interview's over?"

"Sorry, guy. Show's over. But look. I liked that God stuff a lot. We were really starting to cook there for a minute. I'll give you a buzz sometime."

Robert's cell phone rang.

"Yeah, yeah, yeah," he said, then cupped his hand over the receiver.

"Sorry, guy," he told me. "I've gotta take this. Tab's assistant will help you back to the hotel or the airport or wherever you need to go."

Before I left the set, I noticed that Robert was wearing house slippers. Huh. They must have been out of camera range the whole time.

CHAPTER 14

Big D

It was hard to be thrilled with Robert. Off the air, he had hardly paid attention to me. And when our televised meeting was cut short, well, that was a major blow. I sank into a depression. That was always the way. Something bad happens, and then I just can't think about anything else. I obsess. I fixate. Disappointment was the reward for getting my hopes up, and for not taking my Prozac religiously. You go to feeling better and think you don't need the stuff anymore and then there you are.

Hitting my bare fists against things usually helped, except for that time I punched through a cheap closet door and had a tough time pulling my right hand back out. One my knuckles looks wrong, bent to the side a little bit. And since you can't get away with hitting stuff at airports anymore, I headed to Oklahoma. Back home, far from the evils of Manhattan.

Sadie was encouraging. Chin up and all that. She even promised to fly all the way to my house for a weekend getaway. The sun would do her good, she said. Another kiss would do me good, she added.

The more I thought about it, and the more I tried to do my breathing exercises, the more I realized that maybe she was right. My TV debut was brief, but I did get in a few good lines. Robert was still my supporter. And all that breaking news about the Middle East over-shadowed Smirk's stolen footage.

A bonus was the fact that no one knew my last name, at least not yet, and the few who did weren't telling. The woman at the airline counter didn't recognize me. The airline hostess or whatever they're called these days shot me a glance, but I couldn't make out why.

It was hard to read her. She smiled when she first saw me, and she was sweet when she brought me a soda pop. But then she was pretty stern when she ordered me to put my seat into an upright position. I didn't trust her after that.

Anyhow, after a few days, I clawed my way out of the funk, out of the dark hole. The Artist was doing well. On program after program, Robert kept wising up America about my heroic deeds. And he did these online surveys of viewers, asking things like whether they would prefer to have a beer with The President or The Artist. Each time I won, hands down.

The rest of the lamestream media plastered my face on the front pages and on TV shows. Several editorials pressured WNB to release The Artist's last name, and quite a few others demanded my arrest. But the funny thing was that when the press conducted scientific polls, my numbers were nearly as high as in Robert's fake ones. The Artist was getting more and more popular, so much so that a few right-wing governors down south announced that if I lived in their states, they'd pardon me. And a number of state attorney generals flat-out said that they wouldn't prosecute me, including the one in Oklahoma. "It's a free country," he declared.

All told, maybe it was time for me to smirk. I was home free. Hog heaven.

It also didn't hurt that dirt on my victims kept coming out. Turned out that Brewster Jameson had cribbed a few pages of his autobiography from a book written by some old German politician. Cosmo Harrogate was involved in all kinds of questionable financial deals, including a big ponzi scheme. And then, get this, three women claimed that Gerber had groped them. One of them grinned as she told her story, but the other two seemed distinctly unhappy about it.

Now, whether or not they had me pegged as The Artist, my neighbors seemed to avoid me more than ever, which in my book is a win-win no matter how you look at it. But Chet was worried, believing that sooner or later the police were bound to arrest The Artist, regardless of what any attorney general told the press. Careers could be built on the backs of guys like me.

Phone calls brought "Atta Boys" from a couple of pals, as well as one old girlfriend who suggested that we give things another try. Wendy. She was cute, maybe as cute as Sadie, and her voice sounded like she finally had some respect for me. I could almost smell her platinum blonde hair over the phone.

The best word came from Robert Lynch. He was doing a live appearance in Dallas at Reunion Arena. Huge place. And he wanted The Artist to be a surprise guest. No one would know in advance, except his assistant, but he could be trusted, of course. Robert would introduce me, invite me to come onstage, and then share some banter. A bit of conservative back-and-forth.

I wanted to banter, I really did, but I also wanted gas money. Robert agreed, offering to cover all expenses. No salary, because that would be wrong for ethical and maybe moral reasons, but expenses, sure. And charge dinner to the hotel room, no problemo.

Robert hung up the phone while I was still talking. It was a minute or two before I realized that. Now, if phones still had corded receivers that would never happen. You *heard* someone hang up the phone, because that was back when you actually hung up a phone instead of pushing a button. And it was a great sound, second only to the sound of an old phone cord dragging across a desk or table. Those cords gave you something to do with your hands, too.

When my debut in Big D came, it was hot as hell, even at 7 PM. When you went outdoors, it felt like someone had thrown an electric blanket over you, but the heat didn't keep the crowds away. Checking the joint out, I knew that it would be hard to count everyone in there. It was even hard to see them all. They just blended into one big monster with a lot of heads, but then even their heads blurred together.

Sadie was there, too, right in the front row, and she was holding Frog. She discovered him sitting on my hotel nightstand, and never asked anything other than his name. When she held him, she complimented his eyes and announced that they'd sit together at the big show. Forget Wendy and her bottled hair. This gal was on the same page.

Maybe Robert was too. He had paid for Sadie's flight, and he was actually friendly when we briefly shook hands backstage. Then it was showtime.

"Now folks, let me talk to you about The Artist. He's been big news, and he's getting bigger. He is truly a great American. A real, old-time culture warrior."

The crowd cheered.

"Now, let me just say that guys like me are just plain old people. We aren't into high art or opera or all that kind of wimpy stuff. But neither is The Artist. In fact, let's not forget that his name was a media invention. After all, he has told me himself that he just wants to be understood for who he is."

Robert swallowed and shook his head a bit.

"Folks, his real name is Birch. And Birch is an Oklahoman, and he is an American, and he is a great American. He has raised a pitchfork in the air. He has taken up arms against those who would destroy us, and our way of life. And for that, he has my undying gratitude."

The crowds cheered.

"I care about him. And I know all of you do as well."

More cheering.

"And he cares about all of you. Let's all wise up, and let's meet The Artist, in person. He's my surprise guest today."

That was my cue. I waltzed onto the stage, and the crowd went wild. The rooting, the hooting: it was all just one big happy roar. As I live and breathe.

When the audience finally quieted down, they learned everything that my wooden spoon knew by heart. At Robert's advice, I kept the El Camino and Oswald chatter to the bare minimum, concentrating on the need to do repeat life snuffing only when and where it was actually appropriate and, you know, helped the public good and the American Way.

Robert interjected that life snuffing did not constitute the murder of innocent people, which is a crime and has to be dealt with harshly, with life in prison without parole or, better yet, the death penalty, and not just from lethal injection, but from Old Sparky. He went off on a tangent about bringing back the chair, then oscillated back to yours truly.

"Wise Up, America! What this man is doing is preserving our way of life against our enemies, just as the Founding Fathers did all those many years ago. He is a clean stone bearing the brunt of an evil tide. A rock for this age. For all ages. Birch, please, give us some more words of wisdom."

The crowd cheered.

"Can I just say how much I agree with Robert on, well, everything, including my name?"

The crowds cheered and cheered.

"From now on, please just think of me as The Artist Formerly Known As The Artist."

The crowds cheered and cheered and cheered.

I told the crowd that I wasn't very P.C., and that I still liked saying stewardess and stuff like that. They cheered so much that my main point, the one about doing away with the term "serial killer," got lost in the hollers and applause.

Everything went great until I tried to get political. When Robert bashed President Mullins for having an enemies list, I added, "He's nothing more than another Eugene McCarthy."

The crowds didn't boo, but they didn't cheer. Some of them figured out that I had meant Joe McCarthy instead of Eugene, but heck, to some of those old people, Joe was still a hero.

After a few awkward seconds, Robert arrived with reinforcements. "That's what I'm talking about, Baby. That's what I'm talking about. Yeah!"

By that time, his voice was kind of hoarse, causing the "Yeah!" to squeak into a high register. Even though nothing we'd just said made any sense, the audience loved us all the same.

And so did Sadie. Her face beamed when she hugged me onstage, sharing in the final moments of the spotlight. She looked divine strobing in the flicker of millions of camera flashes.

Then Robert got between us, holding our hands and raising them high, just like a referee would do after a boxing match. Maybe they'd start calling me by a new name, like The Champ. Now there's a nickname to be proud of.

If I could just stay out of prison, things were going to be great.

CHAPTER 15

The Fuzz

I'll admit that I was hesitant about pulling the police car over, but courage finally took hold. The El Camino had no siren, so I zoomed right behind him and flashed my headlights. They weren't red and blue, but he cottoned on. Next thing I knew, I slammed my door and strutted up to his window.

Now, let it be said that I have respect for officers of the law and always have. They couldn't protect Oswald, but, look, whatever happened to Tippit, my heart goes out to him. Something tells me he was good people.

As for personal experience with the police, I'll confess to having very little. My driving record was clean. No wrecks. No tickets. In fact, the only time I'd previously dealt with a cop on the road was brief and inconclusive.

I was on a little side street a few years back, in Moore or thereabouts, waiting to wheel onto a larger road. To my left, the downward slope of a hill made it difficult to see if anyone was coming my direction, so I started inching out.

About that time, a police car raced over the hill, its uniformed driver flipping me off. There was no one else in my vehicle and no car behind me, so that middle finger had my name written all over it. Though I only caught a glimpse of his face, he didn't look familiar, definitely not like anybody I'd ever wronged, and I'm always careful to make friends whenever possible. Burning bridges is for suckers.

No, that particular cop must have been having a bad day. Or maybe he was mad that he had to veer over to miss the nose of my vehicle. Call it a misunderstanding and let it go at that.

Knowing better than to make any sudden moves, I kept my hands in plain sight as I approached today's cop car and leaned down to his window. That was when he spoke in a matter-of-face voice.

"This better be good, son."

He must have been in his late fifties, with extra bushy eyebrows, the individual hairs growing in a variety of directions. Gave him an odd look, not David Ferrie-odd, but odd just the same. His voice sounded like he was a smoker, but I detected no pack of cigarettes in his shirt pocket. Maybe age was catching him.

Time to give him the score so that he could appreciate my situation.

We had been about the only two drivers heading north up Sooner Road, my foot pedal carefully maintaining a constant speed several car lengths behind him.

At first, the wiggling I saw out of the corner of my eye seemed to be nothing more than the wind sweeping down the plains and waving the cop's extra long antennae. But that antennae wasn't red.

No, the real shaking came from the reflector that covered half the light bars on top of his car. The blue one was rock steady, but that red one started bobbing up and down, just a tiny bit at first, then more and more, enough so that it damn near hypnotized me.

After a couple minutes, more or less, the left side of the red reflector went straight up, perpendicular to the hardtop, and for a while it seemed content to stay that way, powerfully erect, the bulbs underneath exposed to all creation.

Despite the fact it had my full attention, and I do try to stay frosty, the reflector shocked me when it took flight, soaring off the cop car in my direction. I swerved way too much, but the road was empty and I didn't allow as to how me getting impaled would help matters.

Jerking back into my own lane, I failed to notice where the reflector landed. Probably skipped across the asphalt several times, shattering into a number of smaller and much less useful reflectors along the way.

The cop's chaotic eyebrows relaxed a bit after I finished the story. Then I asked my question, somewhat sheepishly.

"Could I see your license and insurance papers, sir?"

"That'd be Officer Johnson, son. Take my word for it. And step away from my car, please."

Using the word "please" was obligatory. Johnson was no dick, but it was clear that he had balls.

Standing upright after shutting his car door, the fella became imposing, pot belly and all. He calmly looked me up and down with his eyes. His head didn't move at all.

"Say something for me, son."

"Well, I can say anything you like. I mean, I'm just trying to help out."

"That voice of yours sounds familiar. You're not that preacher, are you, son? The one on the television?"

"No, sir."

"What's your license plate number?"

"Oklahoma."

"Figured that was the state."

"Go Sooners," I said, though not very convincingly.

"We best go and take a look at it. You first," he commanded, eyeballing me real close before we started our walk to the back of the El Camino.

"Funny number," he said, after scrawling down "3T-808."

"Yeah, it's a vanity plate."

"You vain, son?"

"Sort of."

"You pay extra for that plate of yours?"

"Yessir."

"What'd it run ya?"

"Not but about twenty or so. It's the number on Humphrey Bogart's car in an old movie I like."

"License?"

For some reason, my left hand instictively went to my left pocket, even though I always keep my wallet in the right. When I finally discovered my license filed between business cards and out-of-date coupons, I produced it.

Johnson sniffed a bit when he blankly examined it, then turned back to his own car. For the first time, he must have gotten a good enough view of his rollers to see that the red reflector really was gone.

"You get in your El Camino there, and I'll be right back with you."

Role reversal. Within a few minutes, Johnson hovered over me, leaning into my car window. Then I placed both hands on the wheel at ten and two, just to put him at ease.

"Birch Barr, huh?"

"Yessir."

"You aren't at home, are you?"

"Well, uhh, no. I'm here."

"You been away from your house for several hours?"

"More than a few."

"Where you been, Birch?"

"Shopping, mainly. Groceries and some Braum's."

"Ice cream?"

"Sherbet. Cherry limeade flavor."

"Yeah, I saw that stuff for sale, but didn't buy it."

I didn't know exactly how to respond, so I just stared straight ahead. Then he showed his hand.

"Birch, I don't mind telling you that I was just inside your house, not more than three hours ago. It's real nice."

I kept staring straight ahead. My upper chest great hot while Johnson began chuckling.

"We really thought you were him."

To keep staring, I fixed my eyes on the bare bulbs atop his cop car.

"It was a tip. Got a warrant and searched your place up and down."

That red reflector sure seemed to be gone, all right.

"You hear me, son? We actually thought you were that assassin."

"Serial killer, you mean."

"Huh?"

"Doesn't matter. Look, I was just trying to be a good neighbor and all, about the reflector. You aren't going to arrest me, are you?"

"Nope." When he said that single word, he sighed, like he was a little disappointed.

"Am I in trouble?"

"No evidence. We tossed your place real good, too."

"Uhh…"

"No gun, no nothin'."

"So…"

"So the detectives there deduced you aren't really him."

"I'm not?"

"Son, you got the sherbet in your car."

"What's that mean?"

"It means you're trying to take the credit, that's for sure, but there's always plenty of crackpots. Even crackpot preachers, goddammit."

"What's the world coming to?"

"For a fact. Take care, son, and quit pretending to be someone you ain't. Now, I'm sure you got plenty of good points on your own without stealing somebody else's life."

After returning my license, Johnson's disorganized eyebrows headed back to his less-than-complete cop car. Once he was out of sight, I hightailed it home. Even if I was in the clear, my stuff wasn't.

Nothing was broken, but everything was a mess.

"I shall not be moved," I promised myself, heading out the back door. Looking up at the stars brought me peace, a kind of glow that lasted until my head titled downward to see the picnic bench on my porch. It was new years ago, but time hadn't been kind to its unvarnished wood.

No one ever sees that table, let alone eats off it, I reminded myself. Deep breaths. In and out, in and out.

After all, I was in the clear, as clear as that night sky.

To celebrate I pulled my new 9mm out of my leather jacket and fired several shots at the stars. 'Course I used the silencer so as not to disturb the locals.

CHAPTER 16

Nuptials

"We should get married, Baby. *Soon.*"

Sadie had a kind of a duckface smile. It was confident, but it was a bit goofy too. Crooked, like she was standing on uneven ground. But she wasn't being goofy when she said those words. They added up to a decree.

Huh.

My mind made some fast calculations, almost like a computer, or at least an old punch card computer, with those nice sounds of a card getting, well, getting punched. Much to my constant regret, those machines were defunct. As far as Sadie goes, I guess my mind had been tallying up pros and cons from the gitgo.

She looked and sounded hot. That's key, right there. And in the sack, she made all my ex's seem tame. Even the way she chowed down on dinner, like a wild animal, was kind of a turn-on, at least when it didn't gross me out. Such a fine line between what turns you on and what makes you sick.

Sadie lived in Chicago. That was cool too. Chicago was as cool as Oklahoma City. Maybe there was even some connection between the two places. Windy City. Wind sweeping down the plains. And being a travel agent meant she could probably arrange badass vacations on the cheap.

Oh, and she was smart. Yeah. That's good. Usually.

Downsides. Hmmm. She was a might bit bossy, always yanking my chain, but on the right day that was okay. I probably needed a bit of discipline. After all, I am an Artist, and kind of a wayward one at that. I need someone to point me in the right direction.

Sadie could have had bigger tits, but so could a lot of women. And you can always buy those. What you do is develop a long-term strategy, starting out with unlimited approval of the current situation. Praise the twins so much that *she* eventually brings up the issue. Then you say, well, now that you mention it, you do want to be as confident as you can be in this life, and if you want to get implants, I'll support you in every way. To the hilt. In fact, as a show of goodwill, I'll even pay for them. I think I've got that much cash set aside, you know, a kind of rainy day, big boobie fund.

More good than bad. More plus than minus. That was Sadie. And hey, she was proud of me. After that event in Dallas, she was definitely proud of me. I was a celebrity in the making. I was a good catch, especially in these trying times.

"Sure. As soon as we can. Let's do it. Let's tie the knot."

Sadie giggled when I said that. She had tied me up just the other evening. Fun, but that hot wax left marks. At least no one else could see them. Sadie was a freak. A super freak.

"Well, where do we want to do it?", she asked. "I was thinking about a wedding in Chicago. Somewhere special, with all the girls from my office there. Then a honeymoon in Vegas."

Of course, the reality was that I didn't have that kind of cash. There wasn't a big boobie fund. There would be, just not yet. I already had bills piling up right beside my stack of maxed-out credit cards.

Maybe I could scare up cash from somebody, but I couldn't try Robert. Time and again he made it clear that he couldn't pay me for TV interviews. He had to stand by his professional code.

No, it was finally time to call Chet. The thing was, Chet had been pretty distant ever since the whole serial killer thing went public. The law and criminality and all that junk.

But Chet also talked about his two kids and bad influences and a bunch of not-so-nice stuff. He didn't like Robert's TV show either. In fact, come to think of it, he was a big liberal, and so his whole attitude of late was probably biased. And even though I don't think he'd ever specifically said anything bad about serial killers, I don't recall him praising them either.

"Look, Birch. I've got some money set aside. I'll quietly give you six thousand to cover a cheap wedding. But you've got to leave me alone from now on. Permanently. That's my price."

I thought about Alice's boobs. Alice was Chet's wife. She never really liked me. I got bad vibes from her. Always had. But her boobs were nice and big. Chet must have squirreled away the six grand for something other than implants. Speed boat, maybe.

Six large was a lifeline, but this sounded like the end of a beautiful friendship. And in my mind, Chet deserved second billing on the special day. Best man. He needed to give a funny toast about The Artist's greatest work being his new bride.

"No way, Jose. You take the money and leave me alone, at least until you get into another line of work. I've got children, for Christsakes."

The dropoff took place at an old Blockbuster Video that had gone out of business. They had taken down the big blue sign off the front of the building, but you could still see the outline of where it used to hang. Now the main feature played out in the parking lot. Chet had arrived first, but he stayed in his car, motor running.

I drove up beside him, driver window to driver window. How I loved handcranking my El Camino window downward. Chet's went down in a flash, fully electric of course. Without saying a word, he poked an envelope at me.

It was pretty thick. Mainly tens and twenties, so it was bursting open. At first I imagined that Chet must have gotten it from an ATM, but the daily limit would probably have been five hundred. Maybe he'd been saving it for quite awhile, sticking in one or two bills at a time and stashing it under his bed.

"Be careful."

That was all Chet said, but he sounded sincere. Then he rolled his window back up.

Chet drove away first, leaving me behind to ponder the good times. Great guy, Chet. He always has been. Alice was clearly the Root of All Evil.

After several phone calls the next day, I managed to book a tiny room at the golf club. Chet's money covered the preacher, a bunch of flowers, a small number of place settings, some champagne, and a few other odds and ends. Oh, and the ring too. I grabbed a cheap one at a little jewelry store on Northwest 23rd, the place that's also a pawn shop.

As for guests, well, Frog was in attendance, safely nestled inside my coat pocket. A couple of Sadie's friends flew in from Chicago, and they paid their own way. She must have bought their dresses. The whole thing was all very nice. Uneventful, but nice. Robert even sent a big bunch of flowers.

It wasn't very long after the "I Do's" that things took a bit of a turn, though.

"What about our honeymoon, baby? When do we fly to Vegas? I've got a new candle I'm just dying to try out. It's supposed to have a pheromone scent. I know it'll hurt so good."

"Well, I don't exactly have any more money, Sweetie."

"You mean I don't get a honeymoon?"

"Well, Chet covered the wedding, but I think he's worried about being publicly tied to me. He thinks it'll hurt his chances of becoming a judge someday or something. He's just going through a phase."

"Have you got some kind of gambling problem or drug addiction that you didn't tell me about?"

"No, no, Sweetie. I'm clean as a whistle."

"But you've been on national TV. And at Reunion Arena. How could you not have any fucking money?"

"Well, you see, Robert Lynch is an honorable man. As a journalist, he can't really compensate me."

Sadie gave me a piercing stare. There was no giggle. No off-kilter smile. Outside of the bedroom, she could be bossy all right. Way bossy.

"All this fame and all this art and no money?"

"Well, the house is paid for, and there's a small trust fund that covers the monthly expenses."

"Listen. If you expect me to stay with you, you've got to learn how to monetize your shit."

"But…"

"What do you expect? Me to support some starving artist? And in some shitty place like Oklahoma? Why the fuck do you think I never go back to Arkansas? You actually expect me to be a travel agent in this godawful place? Listen here, buster. You're taking me places. That's final."

"But…"

"How do you expect to pay for me, and for my kid?"

"Kid? You never said anything about a kid. That wasn't part of the equation. I didn't get to weigh that into my calculus at all."

My teeth crunched a butterscotch into a zillion little pieces.

"Jake's nearly four now."

"Where is he?"

"With my mom in Arkansas, and I promised her that you'll be able to pick up all the medical bills from now on."

"Bills?"

"He's got muscular dystrophy, you insensitive bastard."

"He's one of Jerry's kids?"

"He's *your* kid now. And you better monetize your shit. Quick."

CHAPTER 17

The Feds

Robert leaned his back against a bench in Central Park, his face partially obscured by a large pair of dark, wraparound sunglasses. He wore a cheap T-shirt that advertised Pennzoil, khaki shorts, a fanny pack, and black socks with sneakers. Terrycloth wristbands completed the ensemble.

"You've got the perfect lawyer name, you know that," he muttered, without bothering to turn his head towards the companion seated beside him.

"Jeremy?"

"No, your last name, idiot."

"Stakem? Don't you think I've heard that one before?"

"There's an eighty-sixth time for everything," Robert said with a devilish grin.

"Why'd you decide to meet this guy out here in the open?"

"Because, Jeremy, this is the time when I jog. I don't care if the schmuck is with the FBI. I'm Robert Lynch. And I'm going to jog, goddammit."

Stakem outstretched his left arm, gently made a fist, and turned it upside down while shaking his wrist free from his cufflinked shirt, thus exposing the face of his watch. His children made fun of him for wearing it that way, but Stakem was convinced it protected the crystal. He'd worked hard for that Rolex. And he kept working hard, to pay college tuition for kids who hardly respected him. He charged per hour, so he stood to make more if the FBI agent was late. And more still if he was chatty.

"You told him your attorney would be with you?"

"Didn't phase him."

"This time it's financial?"

Robert shrugged his shoulders in response, then unscrewed the cap of his water bottle and guzzled some H20. When Stakem looked in the opposite direction, Robert quickly popped a couple of suspicious pills and took another gulp.

"Underage woman?"

Robert sighed in disgust.

"The Painter, maybe?"

"The Artist, Jeremy. The Artist."

In disgust, Robert exaggerated his exhale and stretched his neck to the left and right. Then his eyes noticed someone's advance.

"I bet that's him," Robert said, pointing with his water bottle.

"Why?"

"For starters, he's staring right at us and walking right towards us."

Robert motioned to the guy, who quickly produced an ID from his pocket. The agent was federal, but Robert didn't pay any attention to his name. Instead, he slapped both hands down onto his knees and then stood up, with Stakem ripple-affecting the same movement. After the shared intros, Robert laid down the law.

"Let's jog," Robert said, motioning to the asphalt ahead with his water bottle.

The agent turned to Stakem in disbelief, but received no consolation. Stakem was already stretching a wingtip up to his butt, readying for the imminent run.

The agent didn't waste time before unleashing his questions, all of them asked with a voice that shook due to his bobbing head and jogging body.

"Mr. Lynch, what do you really know about him?"

"Him?"

"Birch?"

"You got me."

"What's his last name?"

"Barr, I think. Don't you know?"

"Of course we know. We've known for days."

"Then why'd you ask?"

"Just to see how well you can cooperate with your government, Mr. Lynch."

"Robert, you aren't under oath. You don't have to answer his questions," Stakem interjected. The sound of his wingtips stomping against the pavement nearly drowned out his own voice. It also brought a few glances from passersby, but not very many.

Stakem and the FBI agent were huffing and puffing, out of breath. Their arms moved, but stiffly, due to to the confines of their suit jackets. By contrast, Robert hadn't broken a sweat, even though he wasn't in good shape.

"Shut up, Jeremy. What else do you want to know?"

"You think he's the Artist?"

"Of course he is."

"How can you be so sure?"

"Because I say so."

"Every major crime has lunatics crawling out of the woodwork to take credit for something they didn't do. Publicity whores, that kind of thing."

Robert stopped, causing the other two to abruptly follow suit. He squatted a bit, pushing his hands against the top of his knees. Then, after a deep breath, he took a big drink of water that caused the bottle to make a crunch sound when it squeezed inward.

The agent kept talking.

"There's no record of him buying a gun. He has no gun license. And he certainly doesn't possess the gun used in the murders. Every inch of his house has been searched."

"So, he stole the gun. Or bought it at a gun show. You guys should really keep a better watch on those places."

"Didn't you fight against a bill that would have closed the gun show loophole?"

"And?" Robert asked with disdain, unaware of the contradiction.

"That's not all. Since we learned his name, and trust me, we did before you did, we've kept him under constant surveillance."

"And?" Robert asked.

"Nothing," the agent responded. "Birch is a boy scout. We've interviewed his neighbors and some of his friends, and the most they can say is that they saw him on your show. Oh, and one of them remembered that when he was in fifth grade, he brought his dad's finger to school in a box."

"You serious?" Stakem asked.

"Jeremy, it's an old joke that kids pull on gullable idiots like you. They use catsup."

"Ketchup?" Stakem asked.

The agent cleared his throat, eager to get back to the subject.

"Birch Barr does not fit the killer's behavioral study that we've put together."

"Maybe you guys are screwing up again, like you did with that memo warning you about JFK's assassination before it happened," Robert countered.

"Birch tell you about that?"

"Maybe. Look, can I tell you a story?"

The agent didn't say yes or no, but since Robert always knew the answers to his questions before he asked them, he forged ahead.

"Years ago, I had this apartment, and there was a pond with a little pier, and I was there with a girlfriend. She was a knockout, but a real quiet-type, you know? And I goosed her, and she got all scared and dropped a big set of keys into the water. She was mad, so I went and got a buddy, and we bought an inflatable raft and a rake and we tried to drag the pond, like the area around where the keys fell."

"Robert…" Stakem warned while staring down at his wingtips. The right one looked scuffed.

"I'm talking, Jeremy. So we couldn't find the keys, but while we were looking, out of nowhere this man walks into the pond wearing wading boots up to his crack and he borrows our rake and finds the keys after a few seconds. We didn't even know who he was."

By that time, Robert's pills had taken hold. Relaxation washed over his already confident body.

"I'm not sure how that information helps us," the agent said.

"Of course you don't. That's why I have to explain it to you, because even though I'm against big government, I like you Hoover boys."

"We watch everything and everybody, Mr. Lynch, including accessories after the fact." The agent glared at Robert.

"You're looking through the wrong end of the telescope. You need someone with wading boots to get in there and see the forest for the trees. See, we're in the city, now, but we're also in the wilderness. 843 acres of it, right here in the middle of Manhattan."

"Central Park isn't quite in the middle of Manhattan," Stakem interjected.

Robert and the agent ignored him.

"At present, we have no evidence against Birch Barr, nor do we have any reason to believe he's a criminal mastermind capable of covering his tracks this well."

"But that's just it, isn't it? He's a savant, but an idiot savant."

"Mr. Lynch, you have to believe what you say, don't you?"

"Robert, you don't have to answer," Stakem interjected.

"It's okay, Jeremy."

"Mr. Lynch, it would be quite embarrassing for you if your Artist didn't turn out to be The Real Artist, wouldn't it?"

Robert was finally sweating, so he pointed to the pavement ahead, then began jogging again. The other two followed, heralding the return of shaking voices and stomping shoes.

"Don't you Washington boys get it?"

"Mr. Lynch, I work in the New York office."

"Those three murders were turkey shoots, with no eyewitnesses."

"Actually, Mr. Lynch, we found someone who claims to have seen Jameson's killer from a distance, and his description is hardly in keeping with Birch Barr."

"Maybe *he's* the one wanting attention. Look, I know Birch is a killer. I can see it in his eyes. I know what a killer looks like. You Feds just don't understand the world like I do."

"Mr. Lynch, we have an entire team working this case, and Birch Barr simply does not fit the profile of a serial killer."

"But he isn't, don't you get it? He doesn't do weird shit with their bodies or anything like that. His genius is that he *isn't* a serial killer."

"Mr. Lynch…"

"For once in your life, stop and think. Birch isn't a serial killer. He's just a plain old political assassin, even if *he* doesn't know it. That's why he doesn't keep bloody souvenirs or make lampshades out of their butt skin."

"Robert, I think it's about time we adjourn," Stakem said, halting his half-hearted sprint. On this rare occasion, Robert followed his attorney's lead, and soon the three of them were stationary again, save for their pounding hearts.

"We'll be in touch," Stakem told the agent.

"No. *We* will," the agent advised sharply, wiping the sweat off his neck with a kleenex and turning to walk away.

Robert liked to get in the last word, even if it had to be spoken towards someone's back. His mouth dispensed two cents.

"Birch may think he's a serial killer, but he's really an assassin. He doesn't know who he is, and that's why you don't either."

Without even looking at Stakem, Robert resumed his jog.

CHAPTER 18

On Tour

The advance helped. Some of it paid bills. Some of it went to Sadie's mom. And then there was my appointment with the eye doctor.

I always wore contact lenses, but had begun to worry that my prescription might have changed. Lately my vision wasn't too crisp. A checkup seemed in order, because I wasn't ready to risk laser surgery. That's the kind of thing that you have to wait on for many years in case the first patients end up with bleeding pupils or some other side effect. Plus it cost more bread than I could spare.

The Versatile Speaker's Agency of New York had only coughed up a fifteen grand advance against my lecture tour. But it was cash in hand, and there'd be a lot more where that came from, so they promised. They booked me for nearly that much per talk, and I was already scheduled to appear at a baker's dozen universities. Sadie was smiling, so I was too.

Once again, Robert had come through for me. He used the same agency, and had put in the Right Call to the Right People. That was all it took. That's how the world works for Those In The Know.

"The trick is to practice in front of the mirror. The audience won't hardly be able to make out your face, like they can when you're on the tube, even if they're in the front row. But they'll *feel* your expressions, so you've still got to get them right. Along with the tone of your voice and the pacing of your words."

Thus Spake Robert, and the guy obviously knew what he was doing. He was on TV.

The only thing was, my eyes watered every time I looked into the mirror for more than a few minutes. Maybe it was the new contacts, but the waterworks weren't helpful, especially when I tried to read the speech. Blind in one eye, and can't see out of the other.

Then I tried to memorize the whole thing, spending hour after hour on it. The key stumbling block was Sadie. She kept fiddling with every version that the agency sent over.

The core text was pretty good. Stuff about America and Abraham Lincoln and the NRA and individual freedom and so forth. Sadie wanted something in it about Charles Bronson, which led to a series of drafts that all sounded about the same. Just a few words changed here and there, and some paragraphs cut-and-pasted into different places.

I was unleashed on the home turf. The University of Oklahoma hosted me on a Saturday afternoon, right in Meacham Auditorium. "Local Boy Makes Good." That was what the publicity claimed, but it had a big question mark after the word "Good," as if there really was some kind of question about it.

The fella who introduced me was nice, but he popped off a racist remark about Indian casinos backstage. An albino looking guy with white hair. Everyone has their cross to bear, but I think he wanted to burn his. Once he got to the podium, he read excerpts from a few different editorials, pro and con, but he quoted more nice things about me than bad. I know; I counted.

Come time to talk, I was pretty nervous. And stayed that way, too, but it got better. Somebody once told me that public speaking is right up there with death as far as what scares people the most. Anyway, what was surprising was how small the crowd was. It was almost like the university intentionally booked me on the day of a football game. They wanted me, but didn't want everyone to know they wanted me.

There were a few tough questions, but nothing too difficult. I was nearly broke after the latest round of expenses, so it was easy to sound sincere when claiming that I wasn't in it for the money and had no plans to go commercial. Then I talked about Asia and Lee Harvey Oswald until the albino gave me a cut-off signal.

The best part was the autograph line. These were my people. It was my time. At least that's what it felt like. And Sadie didn't seem to mind the attention that a few of the young gals gave me. One of them was short and buxom as all get out. She wore a low-cut shirt and had a big crucifix hanging around her neck. I had faith that I could see about everything.

One speech down; twelve more to go. Sadie wouldn't let me jam to Cocker on the road, but I put my foot down when she wanted to play her music crap from the, well, whatever the hell the post-2000 era is. Needless to say, I downright refuse to say the term "oughties." I don't appreciate the sound of it.

Overall, the happy couple was happy. Soon the checks really started coming in, and the sex was great. She belonged to me, and I belonged to the world. I scratched that line down on the back of a paper bag so I could remember it later.

Soon Versatile booked even more appearances, including some that weren't on college campuses. A couple were at old theatres that had been refurbished for indie bands and arthouse flicks. So far as I could tell, I was the first serial killer that any of them had ever hosted. And being first had meaning, real deep, Neil Armstrong meaning.

Sure, there were some people who just came out to gawk. Others wanted their five minutes, their chance to ask a question and try to trip me up. But by the third or fourth appearance, I had figured out a couple of standbys. If no good answer sprang to mind, I'd just yell "Wise Up, America," and most of the crowd would go wild, applauding and cheering. That sunk the ship of most would-be troublemakers.

I got booed in Lawrence, Kansas, but who cares. It was Kansas. It was like every liberal in the whole town arrived early to cheat the good folks out of getting a seat. Lots of mean signs too. People can be so ugly. And had bad penmanship. If you're going to write with a big, fat magic marker, learn how to do it properly. I could have drawn some mighty fine moustaches with their Sharpies.

Screw 'em. I was riding high. Versatile was sending a vendor to each show with boxes of The Artist T-Shirts and photos, along with some *Wise Up, America!* paraphernalia. Sadie's favorite was a poster of me looking solemn and brandishing a 9mm. Its caption read "Death Wish."

By the time we got to Humboldt, Sadie changed my speech again. She wanted it to sound more like the real me, so she stuck in words and phrases like "Ungoddamnbelievable" and "Guaranfuckingtee it." I never say those things, but she thought I should, being from Oklahoma and all.

Most of the appearances were fun. A streaker ran behind my podium in Los Angeles. That was something. By the time of San Francisco, I was confident enough to add a little gimmick to my conclusion, hitting a watermelon with a mallet, like Gallagher's Sledge-O-Matic, except I had hollowed mine out in advance and filled it with a gallon of fake blood. The stuff painted the front row when I smashed it, but the conservatives sitting there weren't impressed.

It was at Columbia when everything went really bad, even before it started. For some reason, I got a bigger crowd there than anywhere else. Maybe it was the fact Robert had just done another show about The Artist. Even he had started making the comparison to Charles Bronson. Sadie really did know what she was doing.

Hundreds of folks picketed the Columbia event. Most of them seemed to be Lefties. Typical, whining little bastards. Too much time on their hands, and too much money in their pockets. The endless complaining. It didn't matter, though, because Robert had taught me that they were actually good for business.

But for the first time, there were a bunch of right-wing protesters. Their posters blamed me for not being conservative enough, and for not having shot anyone lately. So both ends of the political spectrum were against the middle, or the Center-Right, which was where I tried to situate myself during the Q&As. I did that because I wanted to appear reasonable.

My talk was accompanied by lots of surface noise. It was as if most folks in the audience were chatting to each other quietly, with all their whispered talk adding up to a distracting roar. A few of them stared at me with admiration, but they were noisy all the same.

There were some intense questions too. Some slimey little gnome with pimples tried to be all self-righteous, correcting something that I had said about John Wayne before launching into an attack about how I was commercializing The Cause. People with smart mouths usually don't say very smart stuff.

Before I could respond, the Gnome kept going, crying about how I had forged a big career out of having only killed three liberals. That got my gander up, but I tried to stay cool. Important things always come in threes, I preached. Magic things even.

I guess I lost most of the audience on that point, with the Gnome cutting me off again, screaming something about RINOs and fraud. That was when things got out of hand.

Was it five people or ten? I couldn't really tell, but several folks charged the stage, and they didn't look happy. Gnome Incorporated. Sadie rushed to my side until one of them grabbed her. Others pawed at me, tugging my clothes. Everyone else in the auditorium just sat and watched what was fast becoming a knockdown-dragout.

At heart, I'll confess that I don't like confrontation. I really don't. Sadie was different, though. She punched the Gnome's associate, and then she clawed at some woman's cheek, her fingernails leaving ouch marks.

I caught Sadie's eye, and it looked tough and angry. Time to ride rough shod over the bad guys, even if I didn't want to. Not surprisingly, the cowardly Gnome brought up the rear of his own regiment. He finally tried to climb onto the stage, raising one foot up so high that I'm surprised his jeans didn't split down the middle. With his other foot still flat on the floor, he unsuccessfully tried to boost himself up. In my imagination, a ripping sound filled the auditorium. In real life, I leaned down to face mask the bastard, but my hand only ended up encircling his nose. Fearing snapshots that would resemble a Three Stooges gag, I released him with a forceful shove. He fell backwards.

Laying there like a stuck pig, the Gnome took a splash of urine yellow on his face, some of it even getting into his mouth. No food or drinks were allowed in the hall, but someone had evidently broken the rules. One of the Gnome's rear-guard compadres must have been wielding a can of Mountain Dew or Squirt or some such pop, but lost grip on it during the melee. Other drops splattered all over the Gnome's cheap T-Shirt, which did not sport a picture of yours truly. Then the wayward can rolled right off my foe's belly.

Displeased with his lowly station, the Gnome's eyes flared. He struggled to stand up and regain his former stature, apparently ready for more of the same.

I reached inside my leather jacket, produced the 9mm, and fired it into the ceiling, sans silencer. Then I waved it in the Gnome's general direction. He was petrified, and the security guards looked ready to pounce. Hell ain't half full yet, brother.

The audience cheered their heads off, even some of the folks who had carried the mean signs. I took a bow while the humiliated Gnome slunk away. Except for a few crazies on the fringe, I had won the crowd without killing a soul.

CHAPTER 19

Infection

I went viral. Full-on, pandemic viral. Everyone wanted a piece of me.

Especially the folks at the Heritage Caucus event. Co-sponsored by the Tradition Foundation, the HC-Con was the biggest conservative event of the year. All the muckety-mucks were there. Now I ranked among them.

Sadie didn't. She stayed home, angry because they only paid my expenses, no salary. That gal was intent on translating me into green.

Me and Tom Trace appeared onstage in a Q&A. On radio, they called him The Magnificent One, "they" being his paid announcer and co-host. A darling of the Alt-Right, Trace brooked no opposition and took no prisoners. The fact he wouldn't go on anyone else's show helped him to accomplish those aims.

When I first made the news, Trace was against me. Now that I made bigger news, he was for me. And to appear like everyday folks, we sat in metal folding chairs. They were cold at first.

Fact is, a lot of the Paleo-Cons boycotted the event, complaining I was a murderer and it was hard to recon-cile that with Family Values. Predictions had it that the crowd would go all Middlebury on me, but they were wrong. More fake news. Some of the folks there were skeptical at first, but not for long. They loved everything we said about the Modern World, how America was always exceptional, except when it wasn't, thanks to the half of the country who voted different than us, the half that wasn't exceptional.

The SRO ate me up with a spoon.

After a good bit of autographs and handshakes, I tried to escape my new friends. My head was spinning, really, with facts about alternate facts, and also alternate facts about facts. I was glad that these people had all the answers. It really was a great Con. But I overloaded on climates not changing and inoculations causing autism. My mind was not only racing, but also crashing. I needed some Me time in the worst possible way.

"Aren't you coming?" Tom asked me.

"I'm heading to the room."

"Nap?"

"Yup."

"You'll miss the dinner."

"I know, but…"

"Sure, next time."

"Oh, say, I did want to ask you."

"Yeah."

"Everyone digs me now, so, you know…"

"What?"

"How does a guy go about cashing in?" I leaned towards him while whispering my question.

"You talking Limbaugh money?" He whispered as well.

"Sure."

"Successful radio or TV show."

"I just don't have that much to say. Not enough for my own show."

"None of us do. That doesn't stop me," he chuckled.

"What about just Ann Coulter money?"

"Books, mainly. Bestsellers."

I nodded yes, even though I was thinking no.

"Catch you later," Tom said.

When I checked out the next morning, I noticed how vacant the lobby was. Then I saw a delivery man outside pushing a hand truck, stacked with crates that said "Pepto-Bismol."

I opened the door for the guy, who nodded with appreciation. That bought me enough goodwill to ask him a question.

"Those really all full of Pepto?"

"Sure are."

He read the puzzled lines on my face clearly.

"Didn't you hear about the outbreak?"

"Huh?"

"Some kind of dinner party last night. Everybody got sick."

"You're joking."

"Ptomaine, maybe, big time."

"I ate in my room."

"Lucky you."

"I guess so."

"I know so," another voice said, coming from behind me. It was a maid pushing a big trolley full of dirty sheets.

"Oh yeah?"

"Some kind of bug must've incubated in the food they ate," she explained. "They're all sick."

CHAPTER 20

Puppets

What a difference a day, or at least a few hundred days, can make. The Artist was no longer a hero to a niche group of politicos, or just a campus rabble rouser, for that matter. I was a celebrity, a real celebrity. A brand, no less.

I had to hire an accountant to handle the money and an attorney to handle the contracts. My name and likeness became registered trademarks, and T-shirt sales were on the up. Paramount Pictures put the kibosh on us using the *Death Wish* tag, but in the end that meant more money in my own pocket. Most of the products just said "The Artist," or "The Artist formerly known as The Artist." Those phrases were trademarked as well.

I tried to interest folks in marketing Frog. Pet rocks were on the verge of making a comeback, I argued, but no one listened.

Chet mailed me a card for my 38th birthday, but you know, I didn't even bother opening it. Once a guy gets famous, he has to be careful of who he hangs with. So many people want something from you, you've gotta to be on your guard. That's where Frog was different. Frog was stone cold.

Sadie was happy. Generally. Well, occasionally, in between the unhappy patches. The crying and the screaming. Jekyll-and-Hyding me all the time. Eventually I learned that bears brought out the best in her. Teddy bears a-plenty. I bought her several of them, giving each a name and a unique personality when I'd make them come alive for her late at night, hiding my hand behind their necks to animate them. Her favorite was a green little grizzly named Roscoe, a real scamp, that one.

She also got excited about travelling, and jawed endlessly about a trip to Europe, even though there was hardly time for that, what with the stand-up routine I was putting together, and my cameo in an action flick that was gonna be filmed in Ohio.

Sadie was busy too. She appointed herself my personal manager, having 18-percent deposited directly into her own bank account. She dealt with most of the phone calls and all of the emails, which I avoided like the plague. She turned down a music video because the band wasn't in the top forty. She turned down a lot of other gigs too. Plus my movie cameo fell through.

Then the unthinkable. As quick as they first came, the flurry of offers slacked off dramatically. A month passed, and the flavor was no longer Birch. So Sadie booked us the first, best proposal that did appear, a high-paying TV commercial.

We took a plane into L.A. the day before the shoot, which tuckered me out. I absolutely hate flying, mainly because I'm kind of scared of heights, and also because 9mm's aren't approved carry-ons. But this time there was no choice.

"Get off it, Baby. You don't need to your gun. It's not like you shoot anybody anymore."

Sadie's lectures were tiresome, but the more I let her have her way, the better the sex. And so through the smog we flew. It looked like smoke from God's cigarette. I said that to Sadie, but she didn't respond. When she wasn't looking, I wrote it down on the back of my boarding pass. It was clever, even if she didn't think so.

A car picked us up at LAX and sped to the Beverly Hills Hotel. That was style. You've gotta give them that. A night on the town, and then an early call on set the next morning.

"Your eyes are so puffy and dark," the makeup girl purred. "We'll have to take care of those."

Pest control. This was a thirty-second TV spot for some kind of pest control, and I was the oncamera talent. There were only a few lines. I sat in the corner reading an old El Camino manual, content that my character didn't have to worry about motivation.

To be honest, I wasn't pleased about the commercial because it seemed small time. Here I had beem climbing a ladder, and this felt like sliding down chutes or snakes or whatnot. Life on the D list. But Sadie insisted. It was a pile of quick cash, and half of it was coming in a brown paper bag. Tax-free money, which seemed a touch illegal, but then again, Robert always railed about Americans being overtaxed. "Wise Up, Birch," Sadie instructed.

The assistant director came over and greeted me, shaking my hand and saying he was so glad to meet me and such like. I think I nodded at the right moments, even though I was pretty sleepy.

"Can I get some coffee, please?"

"No problem. No problem at all."

Sadie stepped on my words, warning me not to drink too much or I'd have to take several pee breaks.

"That's what happens when you get to be 38," she said.

"Bitch, please," I thought. You don't have to say stuff like that in front of other people. It comprised my tough-guy image.

The caffeine felt good coarsing through my veins. It must be like how heroin addicts feel when they get their fix. Forget Prozac. Coffee gave me a surge, an all-consuming charge for a few blissful seconds.

Until Sadie screamed. She was elsewhere on the soundstage, but I knew it was her voice, in all its shrill glory.

As near as I could figure, Sadie had crossed paths with the cameraman. Something about the fact that I wasn't going to get a closeup. The whole thing was going to be a medium shot, except for a long shot when I would draw my gun, or at least a can of the bug spray, and hold it with both hands, arms outstretched, kind of like T.J. Hooker.

The cameraman stormed off the set, but Sadie kept screaming.

The door closed behind him, but she kept screaming.

Several seconds, or maybe even several minutes went by, and she kept screaming.

"He can't hear you anymore, Sweetie," I whispered.

"He may not be able to hear me, but *I* still can hear me. FUCK YOU...FUCK YOU, YOU FUCKING JERK!"

No one seemed too startled by what had happened. It was as if they were used to prima donnas. God knows I was. Sadie was a bell cow. That's all there was to it.

Soon the assistant director joined us, one ear listening to his cell phone and the other listening to Sadie, who was armed with more complaints.

"We've got another cameraman. He'll be here soon. No problem. Okay? No problem. We have no problem."

Within an hour, it became obvious that there was a problem. The replacement cinematographer was nowhere to be found. This time the director came over.

"You know, I've always wanted to work with old style puppets. Not CGI. No, nothing like that. That stuff can still look so fake. No, I mean old style puppets. What are your thoughts?"

Sadie's brow puckered until I said something about Grover from *Sesame Street*. I have heard tell of Elmo, but know nothing about him.

"You see, we've got all the union sound engineers here. That's no problem."

"No problem at all," the assistant director chimed in.

"And so I'm thinking we could record the sound today, and then just do the whole visual side with puppets later."

"Would the puppet look like me?" I asked.

"Yes, of course. That would be the whole point. It'd show your soft side, but not too soft, because the puppet would still be Birch Barr, armed and ready to kill some vile insects, more of America's true enemies."

"What do you think, Sweetie?"

Sadie's face was blank.

"Kind of like Grover, Sweetie."

"Or Kermit, if you will," the director explained.

"It'd be no problem. No problem at all," the assistant director added.

"Of course we couldn't use the name Kermit," the director warned.

"No, we'd use Birch's name," the assistant added.

"Yes, *I* would like to use Birch's name," the director responded, reclaiming his authority by use of the first person.

Sadie slowly smiled her crooked grin. She could imagine it. The red in her eyes transformed into a peaceful blue.

Some non-descript crewmember shouted over to the assistant director, who walked away. By that time, Sadie was glowing.

"Maybe Birch could be a bear, like a walking teddy bear," she suggested, evidently fantasizing about furries.

"But wouldn't that make me look *too* nice? I've got my persona to consider, after all."

"Well, he could be a tough bear," the director replied.

"Like Smokey, maybe," she replied. "With a cool hat and an axe, or a 9mm, or both."

"Smokey the Barr," the directed joked.

Both of them were nodding in agreement when the assistant director returned.

"There's a problem," he announced.

This time it wasn't anything to do with cameramen or closeups or plush bears. No, it was the Minority Whip of the U.S. Senate. I recognized his name after having boned up on political science.

The senator had been shot in the head. Not the back-of-the-side-of-the-head, but between the eyes, and apparently his body kind of jerked real funny before he fell down dead. Or maybe he was already dead by then, and it was his corpse that did the jerking, pre-rigor mortis. There was footage of the whole thing. The Whip Gets Lashed. That's how one conservative website headlined it.

Initial news reports speculated he was probably The Artist's latest canvas. Who else but? That was common sense and conventional wisdom.

Except that it wasn't true. I was soaking up the sun in sunny California.

It must be some kind of joke, or, more likely, an accidental shooting-in-the-face by the senator's own gun, or maybe from a fellow politicians's rifle on a hunting trip.

Either way, it was damn sure big news.

CHAPTER 21

Art School

"So here I am, America, forced to respond to yet another charge against me, and this one really hurts, people, because it isn't about me so much as it's about my father, and family should be off-limits. Sacrosanct."

Robert shook his head slightly in front of the camera, like he usually did while trying to tug at the heart strings. Tab admired that a great deal. Robert could push things to the edge, like an actor who's always on the verge of overacting but never quite goes over the cliff.

"My father burned books. Yes, he did. There. I've said it. That's what all the pinko press and, forgive me, America, the Mother Bloggers on the Left want me to admit."

He licked his lips and shook his head again.

"Wise Up, America!"

His voice grew in strength. It took no prisoners.

"Yes, my father once burned some books."

His voice modulated again. Softer, and with the slightest hint of sadness.

"You see, one winter as a very young man, he could not afford to heat his little house. So he took a pile of old books from his used bookstore back to his home, and he burned them. He burned them for fuel. He burned them for heat."

Robert's eyes began to well slightly. The fact he had a canker sore inside his mouth made it easy.

"These secular scoundrels are trying to tear me down by suggesting that my father was a bad man."

He swallowed.

"Well, my father was a good man. And he burned those books for fuel. For heat."

Then Robert looked upwards, as if towards the sky, as if towards heaven. All he could really see was the top of the soundstage, which was a fairly uninteresting sight, but it was far out of frame. After a healthy pause, he stared into camera two and pounded on his desk with his right fist.

"I will defend my father to the death, America. I stick by the people I care about. I always have, and I always will."

During the commercial break that followed, Robert guzzled some water to replace the sweat. His armpits were wringing wet, so he threw on his sports jacket.

"And we're back. And America, let me tell you, America, we are growing stronger every day. The forces of darkness are on the run. And they are running from us. They are running from the army of us."

His eyes widened, revealing more whiteness.

"The Bleeding Hearts are, well, bleeding, none more so than the Minority Whip's."

Cue devilish grin, followed by light chuckle.

"Now, I know a lot of folks are speculating that here's another baddie offed by The Artist. But today I can announce, unequivocally, that The Artist was involved with an important project in Los Angeles at the time of the assassination. He has assured me himself, through an intermediary, who is his wife, incidentally, that he played no role in that hit whatsoever."

He pointed the index finger of his right hand into the air above him, shaking it slightly to draw attention to his next point.

"Now, what this event tells me is that something important is brewing in this country of ours. If somebody else cracked the Whip, someone completely unrelated to The Artist, then the great movement I started, the great movement that spawned The Artist...it's now much bigger than either one of us."

He breathed in through his nose, then shook his head slightly, up and down while exhaling softly out of his mouth. As he began to talk again, his tongue brushed against the canker sore.

"Wise Up, America! You don't need The Artist to take care of your business for you. You can do things for yourself. Rugged individualism is exactly what our Founding Fathers stood for. And we can stand together as individuals, taking the fight to those who have stolen so much from us."

Robert stood up straight and walked across his set, creating a brief pause for effect. He was wearing slippers, but the camera operators didn't let America see them. His feet were out of frame.

"Let us never forget. If someone came into your home uninvited, my friends, you would shoot them dead with your gun. And you'd be a hero. Speaking for myself, I would shoot them right in the face. And that is exactly the way we have to see our current battle."

The lights dimmed slightly while camera three pushed in for a closeup. Soft patriotic music began to play as a green-screened photo of Mount Rushmore appeared over Robert's shoulder. The running time was about to stop running.

"These people in Washington are invading your homes, and your very minds. They have to be dispelled. What the latest patriot in our cause has proven by ending the Minority Whip's reign of terror is that we can do this.

Together, all of us independent-minded folks can do this. We can take our country back."

Robert's upper lip sank behind his lower front teeth. It made a smack sound as he let it free.

"Remember, we really don't need The Artist. What we need is a whole Art School."

Roll end credits, which rolled quickly and were squished into the left side of the screen while a TV commercial appeared on the right. WNB had only recently started doing that. It saved time, and time is money, particularly on television. But there was Tab's name all the same, even if it had gotten smaller.

Tab was pleased with the Minority Whip situation. A new assassin could drive a wedge between Robert and Birch, which would be no bad thing. Robert might have been right to praise Birch, and it had worked for several months, but the story was getting stale. Old, boring, and stale. All news gets old, no matter how new it is. And there were still regular outcries about putting Birch behind bars.

Of course Birch hadn't made any new news for quite awhile, and some of his career decisions seemed poor, at least lately. TV spots for cheap products were hardly smart choices. At the end of the day, Tab questioned whether or not you can trust a serial killer.

But Birch wasn't the issue today. If anything, he seemed to have outlived his Warholian fifteen minutes. No, the issue today was the culmination of weeks and weeks of trouble. Months, probably. That was why Tab knocked on Robert's office door.

"What the hell is this all about?" Robert was wringing wet, with enough sweat on his body to baptize either himself or some random passerby.

"Robert, please, sit down."

"Fuck you. I'll stand."

"The police arrested the doorman."

"Charles?"

"Yeah, just before you went on the air."

"Well, Charles is a sick little bastard. He's always chewing tobacco on duty, and spitting it into a gross little cup."

"The cops want to interview you."

"About Charles?"

"About the pills he's been selling you for the past year or two."

"Oh."

Tab didn't respond. That single word told him what he already knew.

"Oh. Oh fuck."

"Robert, please…sit down."

Tab buzzed the secretary, asking her to bring Robert a cold bottle of water.

"I'm drowning, here, man."

Tab didn't know what to say. He watched Robert's left palm wipe snot off his nose.

"Tab, what am I going to do. What are *we* going to do?"

Tab sighed. He was genuinely tired. He was the one who needed pills.

"Maybe we can keep a lid on this," Robert whimpered.

"The story's already made the headlines, just in the past hour. Some folks in the office probably leaked it."

"They're all against me. Every last one of them."

"Look, we've got no choice. Today you've got to talk to the cops. Then tomorrow you've got to rip off the Band-Aid."

"Confess?"

"Yeah."

"On the air?"

"Yeah."

"But…"

"And announce you're going into rehab. It's the only way. The D.A. will be looking for a reason not to screw with you, so rehab will probably keep you out of jail."

"And off the air."

"Starting the day after tomorrow."

As usual, Tab was right. The cops didn't arrest Robert. The meeting consisted of Robert autographing books for them. They shook his hand. They laughed at his jokes. And they asked him what The Artist was really like. It was about the same as any other book signing.

But the next day at the studio was different. More of a waking dream. Everyone who saw Robert smiled politely, and most of them said, "Good Morning," but they tended to avoid his eyes. They all knew, of course, and most of them were delighted. Robert was the news, more than ever before, but this time he wasn't controlling it.

Tab looked different too. His eyes were tired, and he was wearing blue jeans, which was odd. Robert didn't even know he owned a pair. Tab didn't glance away from Robert. In fact, he looked Robert directly in the eyes while handing him a prepared script to read.

"No, Tab. Let me do this one my way."

"Like always?"

"Yeah, just like always."

Cue credits and theme song.

"America, let's talk."

Robert pursed his lips. His eyes appeared sincere, even if dark and swollen.

"America, I have to announce that, as of tomorrow, my good friend and colleague Belle Hewitt will take over this show on an indefinite basis. You all know Belle from her guest appearances on this program, as well as from her own radio show *Beating Back.*"

Belle was popular with the right-wing, and so she was a good sub for him. She had a husky-sounding voice, like she had been yelling for an hour or two straight. Many years earlier, Belle had posed for some nudie magazine, which, after having learned the error of her ways, gave her the right to tell other people how to run their lives. It also gave her license to wear low-cut blouses without seeming slutty.

Of course there was the danger that Belle was so good that she'd steal Robert's TV thunder, but he couldn't worry about that now.

"You see, America. I've got to take some time for myself. This time I've got to Wise Up. The past few months, the past several months, fighting our enemies has taken such a toll on me that I was running low on energy. The exercise wasn't helping, and to be perfectly, one hundred percent honest, I've been running on fumes."

His head shook up and down a bit.

"You see, I needed a pick-me-up, and a really awful fellow, who I've just learned is a dirty Commie, incidentally, gave me some pills, and, to be perfectly honest, which I always am, of course, they helped give me the energy I needed. They became my fuel, which I desperately needed."

He looked downward for a moment, and then up again, directly into the camera.

"Pills for fuel. For heat."

Cut to commercial.

"And you are out," the director said.

CHAPTER 22

Many Happy Returns

"Oh god, this is such a nice place, Baby. Would you just look at those paintings on the wall?"

With her freshly-dyed black hair and her skimpy, bright orange dress, Sadie was beaming. Her smile was full-on. Not crooked, but level and wide. It was her birthday, and exactly the kind of scene she loved. Beverly Hills. Ritzy restaurant. The best table in the joint, with everyone eyeballing us.

This was probably why Sadie had chased Representative Gerber. I thought of that often. She wanted the Good Life. I could only wonder why she ever went for me. Was it the fact I had killed some people, or because she thought I had some money? Maybe it was both.

"Excuse me, sir, I know this is highly irregular, but may I please present you with the chef's hat?" The waiter looked slightly embarrassed as he rested it on the table and gently pushed it towards me.

"Am I supposed to wear this?"

"Very funny, sir. No, you see, our chef…he's a very big fan of yours, and he'd love for you to autograph it for him. As you know, we pride ourselves on being a safe haven for the glitterati, but it would really mean a lot to him."

"Sure thing. Do you have a pen? 'Course, I could sign it in blood."

I stared at the waiter right in the eyes when I spoke that last line. Kind of got him back for checking out

Sadie's tiny tits when he seated us. With no bra, if she moved the right way in that dress you could see the sun and the moon.

"What's wrong with you, tonight?" Sadie asked savagely.

"Nothing, Sweetie, nothing. Just tired. Here, why don't you open your gifts?"

Sadie tore open the packages like a grizzly bear ripping open a man's chest.

"Oh my god! Oh my god! Oh my god! Look, everyone! Look! Would you just look!"

When she held up her new jewelry, an old lady at the next table smiled and clapped a couple of times until her even older escort frowned.

Snatching all four pendants out of the box, Sadie didn't even notice the elderly couple. There was a large diamond pin shaped like a cat ready to pounce, and then there were three smaller pins shaped like mice. The whole thing looked awesome on Sadie's chest, like a blinged-up cartoon chase.

"Oh my god! Oh my god! Oh my god! Look, everyone, look!"

"Her name's Cherry," I whispered.

"So cool. Oooh. So hip," Sadie cooed.

She lifted her new pet rock and examined it from every possible direction. I had spent a fair bit of time on it, painting eyes and gluing on a lace skirt. Cherry was for Sadie, but, to be honest, she was for Frog.

"You really are an artist," she said. "Look, I've been wanting to say just how much I love you."

I smiled, but just for a moment.

"What's wrong, Baby?"

"Nothing, Sweetie, really."

"I know I can be a handful sometimes. My mother always tells me I need to quit being so bossy."

I tried to smile, but avoided her eyes.

"All right, all right. Look, it was really wrong of me to make you sell the El Camino, and to store your books in the attic without asking. You were right when you said they were all organized on the shelf so well."

I held her hand and squeezed it tightly.

"And you've been so good letting me send money to Mom. It's helped Jake so much. We've got to go visit him, you know. I haven't seen him since we got together. You really should meet him."

"I will, Sweetie, one of these days. Real soon."

The waiter reappeared with the champagne. Another waiter held a dozen roses, which I had asked them to deliver right after Sadie opened her presents. Once again, everyone in the joint looked, and once again, Sadie glowed like a luminary on Halloween. By contrast, my smile must have turned upside down.

"Oh, cheer up," she commanded. "It's my birthday for god's sake. It's *my* day."

The first waiter popped the champagne cork.

"I'm sorry. It's nothing to do with you or Jake."

"Well?"

"It's Robert. And what's-her-name. That gal filling in for him."

"You're mad because she's talking shit?"

"That I'm a phoney? That I've gone into early retirement? Yeah, exactly."

"Shoot someone, then."

"Well, it's tougher than you think. But it's not just that."

"I knew it was me."

"No, no. It's Pandro."

"I can't believe you're worried about him."

"Well, Belle is really talking him up, like he's special or something."

"He's the new flavor of the month, that's all."

"Have you watched all those tapes?"

"I can't believe you still use a VHS recorder."

"I like the sound of the top load when it pushes down and locks into place. But that's not the point. Robert was promoting this idiot right before he went on leave."

"To rehab."

"Don't you see this is a problem? I've got major competition now."

"Forget about it. Pandro's the phoney."

"Damn straight. He's only killed one person. The Minority Whip just *seems* more important than anyone I shot. Cosmo was the man."

"Baby, most people just don't understand politics like you do."

"It's not even that. To be a serial killer, you have to have three. *Three.* And that idiot just has one."

"I know," Sadie said, "I know," and she did, because I'd taught her that very point on many occasions. She looked down at her champagne wistfully, watching the seemingly endless number of bubbles pop after reaching the surface.

"And these things take planning. Careful planning. Strategy and tactics."

"But Baby, you told me you chose your first victim without thinking. Like random."

"Don't ever bring that up in public," I whispered loudly. "Besides, even if it was a bit random, it's because I'm a great artist, and great artists improvise."

"I told you not to go on that program last week."

To be fair, Sadie had warned me right before I appeared on *Meet the Press*. They asked me what I thought, and I told them. I flat-out said that one assassination doesn't count, that three was the magic number. And I declared that Pandro isn't a serial killer's name, not a good one, anyhow. But Chuck Todd cut me off, playing an old clip where I had complained that the term "Serial Killer" wasn't politically correct. He used me to catch myself.

Then the *Meet the Press* roundtable dissected my interview. Sour grapes, one believed. Jealousy, another argued. A third went so far as to psychoanalyze the whole situation. He claimed that my day was done, mainly because my message had become confused and contradictory. Hence my inactivity of late. And hence my political impotence.

Daily tracking polls had revealed a marked dip in The Artist's popularity, particularly with right-wing retirees and soccer moms. And that old bag on *Wise Up, America!* had a field day. She wouldn't even take my phone calls.

"Oh my god! Oh my god!" Sadie shouted, causing the old woman at the next table to scream. For the first time, the old man echoed his date's emotion.

A guy wearing a rubber mask charged into the restaurant. In his left hand, he held an odd-looking pistol, like an old Nazi Luger. He used his right hand to tug at the mask, presumably to help him peer through the eye holes.

After running into a table and knocking over the chair on the other side of it, he finally spotted me.

"The paparazzi ratted you out," he shouted.

Even at a glance, I knew that his mask was supposed to look like Pandro, what with the slicked black hair and pencil-thin moustache. Good god, that little fucker must have hustled to get a licensing deal so quick. That, or the company bootlegged the masks into production without his permission. Either way, it meant that Pandro really was the new flavor of the month.

The Mask pointed the gun directly at my face and pulled the trigger. I braced for the bullet, trying to maintain and stay cool, but there was no sound. No gun-fire at all. Instead, a little flag popped out of the barrel that declared, "Pandro's Number One." At that very moment, a camera flashed. The Mask had a compadre.

"Made you flinch," the Mask laughed, his words muf-fled through the rubber.

I grabbed my steak knife, but Sadie reached across the table and seized my wrist.

"Don't ever shoot down, Baby. Only shoot at those above."

The Mask dashed out of the restaurant almost as quickly as he'd entered. The whole scene unfolded in just a few seconds, though I feared it would be replayed over and over again on YouTube.

With the knife still in my hand, I wiped sweat off my forehead. Then my head snapped to the side after glimpsing the waiter in my peripheral vision.

"Check, please."

I hadn't bothered to ask Sadie if she was finished. I knew she was. She had attacked her chicken so fast that I never knew whether or not it was boneless. All the food on her plate was gone, leaving no trace that anything had ever actually been there.

CHAPTER 23

Cheerful Angst

The whole damn scheme sounded like performance art. And performance art is for chumps and wusses. Stinks to high heaven.

"But won't you please listen, for just a moment, Birch? Please. At least give the idea a chance," my new agent pleaded.

"We have your best interests at heart. This is good for your brand," the agent's assistant added.

I stood while all the others sat. I looked at my publicist, who said nothing. Then I stared longingly at Sadie, who tilted her head and closed her eyes slightly, giving me a mean glare, a silent reminder of her pep talk earlier that morning. As my manager, she advised me in the strongest possible terms to sign the contract.

"Look, if we're at an impasse here, let's go back to talking about a social media blitz. Facebook, YouTube, all that," the agent said.

I paced the floor, my silence being a loud reminder that I wasn't interested in the internet. Blogging? That was for suckers.

"Your numbers are down," the agent said.

"Way Down," the assistant added, tentatively.

"And Pandro's are up. So we've got to inject your career with something new, something big," the agent said.

"How about shooting Pandro in the back-of-the-side-of-the-head?"

"Baby, we've talked about that. It would just look vindictive," Sadie told me.

"Very vindictive," the assistant added.

I looked at my publicist, who said nothing. She was cute, but close-mouthed.

"You know the rumor is that the guy who came into the restaurant wearing that Pandro mask really was Pandro," I argued. "It was a double bluff."

Sadie rolled her eyes.

"Have you even looked at the data that we emailed you?" the agent asked.

I spit out an ill-formed word that Sadie stepped on.

"Birch doesn't check his email. But I read all of it. Did I ever tell you guys about the time Birch went up to a cashier at a coffee shop and demanded his 'free wiffy,' like it was a free gift or something?' He saw 'Free Wi-Fi' and didn't even know what it was."

The agent, assistant, and publicist ignored her, which I appreciated to no end.

"Birch, the thing is, these days your numbers are strongest with the 13 to 25 crowd. That's where you really haven't lost much ground. A majority of them still think you're the bomb," the agent said.

"And that's why we need to target them," the assistant added.

"With my gun?" I said, asking a question that was completely ignored. No chuckle, no nothing. Glancing at my publicist caused her to stare at her own feet. They looked good in her funky platforms, what with her blue toenail polish and all.

"Can't you see it, Birch? Up in lights. Your name. And I'm talking big, bright lights. New York City," the agent said excitedly, his voice increasing in volume.

"The Big Apple," the assistant added with a smile.

I sighed, but Sadie spoke over the last bit of my exhale. "Birch isn't fond of New York."

Or anywhere east of the Mississippi, I thought to myself while staring at nothing in particular.

"We aren't talking about measly universities," the agent said. "Really, you've got to get out there, ahead of the ball."

"And this will land us our reality TV show, for sure," the assistant added.

"Can we manufacture some pinback buttons that say The Artist?" I asked.

"Teens aren't that into buttons anymore," the assistant said.

The agent spoke louder, talking to me while watching the assistant. "Sure thing. Whatever you want. I mean, all I've got to do is pick up the phone and set the wheels in motion."

Again I looked at the publicist, who again looked at her feet. She resembled Velma from *Scooby Doo.*

"Baby, this would be kind of wonderful," Sadie said, her voice nice and breathy, as if she was already nibbling my ear.

"Kind of? Those two words are pretty shaky qualifiers. Anyhow, the whole thing just seems strange, and maybe even cruel. Like not nice at all."

"But that's the genius of it," the agent said. "It'll put you out in front. Pandro doesn't even have a second kill yet, and you'll already be in another league, playing another game."

"A new game," the assistant added.

"And Baby, Lee Harvey Oswald worked on both sides of the fence, didn't he?"

"Not really. The anti-Castro stuff was just a ruse."

"But Baby, you've always told me that your heart isn't really in politics."

This time it was me who gave Sadie a mean look. That information was just between the two of us. State secrets.

"None of that matters, Birch. After all, it's not like you're switching sides, here," the agent said.

"Not at all. Heaven forbid," the assistant added.

The publicist looked at me, but not into my eyes.

"Well, young people are rebels," I said, reconsidering the offer, "and they do hate authority."

"Well, maybe. We don't have figures on that," the agent said.

"Not at hand," the assistant added. "What we do know is that the college kids are increasingly conservative, and they still seem to look up to you."

"They *do* look up to you," the agent said, correcting his colleague.

I glanced at my publicist, who remained blank-faced. Then I spoke again.

"Isn't this crap against the law?"

"Manhattan has just passed an ordinance that makes doctor-assisted suicide legal," the agent said confidently. "It only requires the consent of the victim and the doctor. That's it. Nothing else."

"But you can't even buy a Big Gulp in New York anymore," I countered.

"They rescinded that ordinance, even before Bloomberg left office," the assistant replied.

"Word on the street is that the assisted-suicide law will probably be amended soon, made more complicated. That's why we've got to act now, while it's all nice and legal," the agent said sharply, restaking his claim to the conversation.

"But I'm not even a doctor."

"Yes, you are," the agent argued. "We bought you two degrees. One is a Ph.D. in Divinity, and the other is a med school diploma from Bolivia. And look, the victims we have in mind really want to check out."

"They're just asking for it," the assistant added.

"The hell you say," I said in disbelief.

Sadie stared at me again, her eyes widening and her head bobbing an inch or two forward, as if to offer a silent "Duh." So I gave in.

"Okay, okay. Let's go for it."

From that point on, I tried to be a good boy, studying my script carefully. Most of the show was action, but they did write me several lines, and gave me some buzzwords to use as filler. On the one hand, they discouraged me against improvising about El Caminos and Joe Cocker. That palaver was okay for universities, maybe, but not for discriminating audiences like teenagers at concerts.

Practicing in front of the mirror, I stumbled over the dialogue about President Mullins being a shithead. That seemed kind of strong. At the end of the day, I hated profanity, even if I had begun using more and more of it since my wedding day.

"Do I have to say S-head?"

"The crowds will love it." The agent or the assistant said that. I forget which, but I'm confident it wasn't my publicist. She remained tight-lipped, but I sure liked her lipstick. Best not to tell Sadie.

Radio City Music Hall is a great place, if you've got to be in New York. As soon as we arrived, we spotted advertisements for the show plastered everywhere around town. The agent was thrilled to learn that it was a sell-out crowd. The assistant most likely agreed.

Cheerful Angst opened for me. They were one of the hottest up-and-coming bands. A mix of death metal and bubblegum pop, their songs featuring politically relevant lyrics that expressed the discontent of America's youth.

The words of their songs didn't rhyme, which prompted music critics to say they were important. Cheerful Angst was the Real Deal, caring more about their cause than smoothness of verse. Rock on, I thought, lying to myself.

When the time came, a light show drenched the auditorium in weird colors while a recording of Asia's *Heat of the Moment* blasted out of every speaker in the joint. That was my key victory, a final condition to sign on the dotted line.

Then a loud, booming narrator made my presence known.

"Sportraits, starring The Artist formerly known as, and still currently known as, The Artist."

I moseyed onto the stage, tripping over a cable or something, but I recovered quickly, all nonchalant like. I don't think anyone noticed, although the spotlight on me was so bright that I couldn't tell for sure. If there were chuckles, the applause drowned them out.

My speaking coach had taught me well. I was nervous, so I walked around while speaking. Stage left to stage right and back again. Not manically, but methodically. One body had to fill the arena, at least for the first part of the show.

It was a good speech, full of jokes and hip conservative chat and stuff about putting things right, some of it left over from my ill-fated stand-up routine. A bit rude, but not Milo rude. And it was short, which was important. I reckon I had come a long way from my first university gig, but there's still only so long you can hold a youthful crowd in the palm of your hand.

Amazingly, there were no hecklers in the audience, at least not any that heckled out loud. I did get a few unintentional laughs after calling the President "jive-assed." The language was out of date, but it beat saying S-head.

There were also a few groans when I went off the reservation with a little joke that I made up about Pandro, but there you go. It felt good to denounce him right in front of the world, or at least the tiny segment of it that bought tickets to my show.

Besides, it led nicely into the next round of music started. This time it wasn't Asia, but it was fairly dramatic, all the same. Intense orchestral stuff. The gimmick was finally underway.

The booming narrator returned, heralding "For the First Time Evers" and that sort of thing.

One curtain went upwards while two stone cold foxes pushed a large canvas onto the stage. It was on wheels, and they did this cute thing where they twirled it 360 degrees before moving it into position.

Three more hot chicks entered from the opposite side of the stage. Their long legs marched in step to the music, almost like they were in a parade. One carried a table against her tummy like she was a cigarette girl. The second held a little jeweled box in both of her hands, which she placed on the table. The third had a stool, which she positioned right in front of the canvas.

The five of them lined up, with arms on each other's shoulders. They took a bow and then Rockette-ed off the stage in time to the music. All the while, lasers beamed every which way but loose.

It was all very magic show, to the extent that the volunteer was seated on the front row of the audience. A little geek of slight build, and boy, did he eat up the applause.

Only a few weeks earlier, the Geek had announced on Facebook that he would commit suicide for being bullied at school. Instead, he changed his mind and agreed to become The Artist's first official Sportrait. Convenient, and generous as all get out.

Though he was despondent, the Geek followed my instructions to the letter. He easily found his way to the stool, climbed on top of it and took a bow without stumbling. That's talent. The kid had talent, and balls, really, far more than whoever bullied him. God, I hate bullies.

Louder music charged the already electric air when I carefully opened the jeweled box. Inside was a gold plated 9mm that shimmered in the ever-changing lighting scheme. I prayed that the photographers had star filters on their lenses. Then everything went dark except for a single white spot that illuminated me and the Geek.

After shaking his hand, I motioned for the Geek to pivot on the stool, turning until the back-of-the-side-of-the-head was proscenium-arched to the crowd. Some of that was about consistency, but more of it was about building suspense. Then I squatted down to get just the right angle on things. I wanted to put a little English on whatever body parts were about to move. Just a little bitty bit.

The shot reverberated. It was loud, but not so loud that it drowned out the Geek's Krr-Splat. Of course the audio crew had secretly pushed in a microphone right behind the canvas in anticipation of the impact.

Sportrait Numero Uno. Lots of blood, and some good chunks too. Once it dried, the canvas would have some real texture to it.

I rested the gun on the table, stood up, and made a dramatic turn back to the audience.

There was a brief pause, or maybe a long pause. Pauses in public work outside of the space-time continuum. Anyways, I slowly lifted my two arms into the air and opened them extra wide, as if to accept a hug from the audience. They had never seen the likes of me.

The dam burst. If there was clapping, you couldn't hear it over the loud cheers. The crowd went wild. Success. And it was all wonderfully and completely legal.

Rolling Stone put me on its cover that week. My agent had said that young people don't read magazines anymore, but, hey, it was *Rolling Stone.*

The critics were befuddled, expecting to find that The Artist had no smock, but there I was, standing tall in my boots, taking in every bit of the love that was truly given. The canvas would later be auctioned to the highest bidder, and the proceeds would go to charity. Who could complain? I mean, you can't beat that with a stick.

The *New York Times* was appalled, calling the show an orgy of vulgarity, reaching so far into the depths of Hell that it could have produced a demon, but then, they said, that would have been unnecessary, because the demon was already there in the person of an alleged artist whose sportrait was, in fact, marred by both poor taste and even poorer composition. True, most of the Geek's head blew onto the top half of the canvas, but some blood eventually dripped downward. Oh well. What can you expect from fake news?

Of course the best response came from Pandro, who had no response. The press said he was unavailable for comment.

CHAPTER 24

Chicken Fried

I drove the car, mainly because I didn't want to go where I had to go.

Johnny Q. Law had reared his ugly head again, right smack in my own backyard. Garvin Strickler was District Attorney for Oklahoma County, in which resided me and all four walls of my home. Sadie and Frog and Cherry as well, though they weren't in imminent jeopardy, not unless Frog could be named a co-conspirator.

And Garvin, or Mr. Strickler, or whatever you'd call asshat, well, he wanted me to drop by his office. That's what he said. Or at least that's what Strickler's secretary told Sadie. It was going to be an informal chat, which meant that it was going to be a formal inquisition.

Returning to Oklahoma after the whole Sportraits to-do, I wanted nothing more than to sink into my couch and eat pizza horizontally. Some soda pop too, which you can in fact drink while reclined, so long as you have a good, bendable straw. But up and comes this nonsense.

It was probably inevitable once I was no longer the darling of Robert Lynch and Co. 'Course I told myself that I never wanted to be anyone's darling, except Sadie. And even then there were days.

"Shit, Baby, Strickler's scared of you."

I didn't respond.

"They've got no evidence."

I breathed in deeply through my nose, then out through my whistle-shaped lips.

"You're still too popular for these clowns. It's like your untouchable."

I exercised my right to remain silent.

"You don't believe me?"

"Probably I don't."

"Fuck you, too, then," she said in disgust.

The two of us didn't speak for several minutes, in part because we had butted heads and in part because I was concentrating on the road. It was an overcast day, sprinkling off and on. In order to see, I had to squint between the damp and the dry raindrops on my dirty windshield.

Sadie sighed, shook her head, and stared out the passenger window. Presumably she pouted because I had yet to turn on the wipers. But I knew I couldn't do that. The windshield wasn't quite wet enough for the wipers to work, and I hadn't gotten around to refilling the wiper fluid. Fixing the problem would make it worse.

And so our drive to the informal chat became quite formal in its own way, stiff and stuffy and thoroughly unpleasant. I thought about sneaking a peak at Sadie's mood ring, but I already knew its color.

After locating Strickler's office building, it took awhile to find an empty space in the parking garage. It took even longer to see Strickler. I assumed the guy kept us waiting intentionally. Just to make me sweat. Just to jack with me.

Yes, we had an appointment, I told the secretary, who then told another secretary. Neither was very polite. The first was a big ole heifer. The other was pretty, but in an icy kind of way that didn't do her any favors.

Trying to read an old magazine, I worried that the weather might be taking a turn for the worse. At first I thought I heard some thunder, but it was just my stomach rumbling. Then I looked down at my feet. I had accidentally worn one black shoe and one brown shoe. Lordy. That was the second or third time I had done that lately. I had also left the keys in my front door one night.

"Well, now, there he is," Strickler said while walking towards me, stating the obvious in typical Oklahoma style. "Let me shake your hand there, Artist."

While exchanging pleasantries, Strickler quickly inspected Sadie up and down.

"Where have you been hidin' this little filly, Artist?"

"Oh, you know."

"Should make her a part of your new show. She's about as purty as they come," Strickler remarked with a smile. He winked at her too, or at least that's how it looked from where I was standing.

Sadie maintained eye contact with Strickler, her eyes glaring ever so slightly, like she was about to swat a mosquito. She didn't like him, or his bolo tie.

But Strickler didn't notice, intently gazing passed us to the hallway outside his secretary's office.

"Say, why don't the three of us walk over to greener pastures?"

"Huh?"

"There's a nice big conference room across the way. Good leather seats, you know. Plenty of room to talk. And eat."

Strickler led the way, with me and Sadie making brief eye contact as we followed. I raised my eyebrows, as if to suggest that maybe things were going to be okay. Sadie was unimpressed.

Once we were inside the room, Strickler closed the door and pulled out one of the chairs for Sadie. I sat down too, mentally agreeing that the seats were made of first-rate leather. Anybody could see that.

"Probably you're both wondering why I asked you here today," Strickler said as he sat himself down. "Now, as I tried to say, or have my secretary say, that this isn't a meeting. No sir. This isn't a meeting."

"But we are meeting. We just met, and now we're meeting in a meeting room," Sadie said sharply.

"Let's call it a get together, a quick confab between friends."

"We just met," Sadie reminded him.

"Acquaintances, then."

At about that moment, some guy knocked on the conference room door and opened it without waiting for anyone to invite him inside. He wheeled in a pushcart.

"Hope ya'll are hungry," Strickler said.

The guy with the cart placed silverware and covered plates in front of all of us, then offered tea or coffee. Real nice. I asked for sweet iced tea, but the guy gave me regular with some sugar packets and a disposable wooden stir.

"Figured we could do a working lunch," Strickler suggested, "if that's all right with you, Artist. Didn't know what ya'll liked to eat, so I ordered chicken fried steak all round. That okay?"

"Sure thing."

"That's good," Strickler chuckled. "No vegetarians here then."

"No, no. Nothing like that."

"Hah! Carnivores, each and every one. I knew it. Well, good. You know, if I ever go full-on into politics, like as a senator or something, I figure I should pass a law keeping vegetarians out of this here state."

"Sound good to me," I said hesitantly.

"That cream gravy looks pretty greasy," Sadie complained after unveiling her lunch.

"Yup," Stricker agreed. "But they don't usually make cream gravy with cream, now do they?"

Even though he was fairly trim, Strickler clearly had enough ass on him for any two decent people.

"So…you're gonna arrest Birch, aren't you?," Sadie asked.

"Now just hold on there, little lady."

"Answer the question," she commanded.

"Whoa, Nelly," Strickler said.

"Yeah, whoa, Nelly," I added.

"Why are we here then? Hopefully it's not for these rotten mashed potatoes," Sadie groaned, leaving her fork stuck upright in a pile of them.

"I guess maybe they aren't too good at that," Strickler said. "Taste instant."

I didn't know which of the two of them to look at, so I ogled my own plate. Seemed like a bad idea to eat potatoes given all that had just been said, so I sawed off more of the tough chicken fry.

"What do you think of the food there, Artist?"

"Meat's pretty good."

"Good enough to slop grandma," Strickler chuckled.

"Hardly," Sadie snapped.

"Now, let's think about this whole thing, here. Calmly, now. We're all friends here."

"We just met," Sadie reminded him.

"The upshot is that some folks are calling for your head these days, Artist. Not me. Not yet, anyways, but that wind out there can blow in different directions real quick." As he said that, Strickler unknowingly dragged the cord of his bolo tie through his gravy.

We said nothing in response.

"Enough wind starts blowin' and a few other things go the wrong way and, well, you've got yourself a tornado on your hands. Some of the law dogs in these parts are having a major rethink, maybe that you are the one and only Artist, and maybe, just maybe, mind you, they can finally dig up some evidence to prove it."

"Birch can handle anything that comes up," Sadie warned him.

"Take no guff. That's my motto," I chimed in.

"You aren't packin' today, are you, Son? That'd be a crime, you know, to bring a gun onto these here premises."

After reassuring Strickler, I thought about how I liked being called "Son." It beat "Sir" all to pieces, because you just don't want folks to start calling you "Sir" while you're still thirty-something. Sounds too middle-agey.

"Where were we? Oh, yeah. Now, I don't think it'd surprise anyone at this table that some folks are sayin' The Artist has got way too big for his britches. Tread lightly, Artist. That's all I'm a-gonna say."

"Perhaps you could flesh that out some more. It's hard to understand what you're really getting at."

"That's all I'm a-gonna say," Strickler repeated.

Out of nowhere, the dark clouds inside the room gathered quick and fast. Total downpour. Sadie burst into tears without any real warning. She didn't raise her hands to her eyes, let alone a tissue. She just let it all hang out, at least until she stood up. That caused her chair to fall backwards. When it hit the floor, she stormed out of the room.

I couldn't see my own face, but it must have looked completely shocked. Some sound came out of my mouth. Not a word. Not even a clearly articulated "Oh" or "Uhh." More like an "Ope."

Putting my hands into my pockets, I nervously rustled two or three butterscotches and then made up my mind to leave. When I started to turn towards the door, Strickler spoke.

"Say, Artist, it ain't that I don't like you. Just don't make me do my job…if you haven't already."

I looked at Strickler, but my brain was staring at Sadie, who was presumably marching straight to the parking garage.

"Wait just a second here, now," Strickler smiled. "Can you sign an autograph before ya go? It's for my kid."

CHAPTER 25

Train Schedules

"You sure you're ready to get back on board?" Tab's voice sounded hesitant when he asked that question.

"Back aboard Robert Lynch's Train of Truth? It is my toy train, after all."

Robert appeared pale. He had gained some weight during rehab, but instead of fattening him up, it just looked like loose extra skin, almost as if it was melting down the side of a thick candle.

Over the years, Robert and Tab had spent a good deal of time in the little coffee shop on the ground floor of their building. The Caffeine Scene. Nice place, in a grubby, not-so-nice sort of way. Its primary advantage was that it had booths, the leftover interior design of a deli that had once operated in the same location. In fact, the booths probably dated to a noodle bar that operated long before Robert ever had a TV show.

Booths are generally rare commodities in coffee shops. Tables, sure, but not booths. A real bonus, because you get that extra little bit of privacy. Here media moguls could plot strategy, towering over the little people even while sitting on the ground floor.

Plus, the booth gave Robert some cover, a minor amount of visual protection against prying eyes when he poured booze into his Americano. Brunch in a cup. He didn't always drink, but he had more of a taste for the stuff these days. When he was popping the pills, he always felt dehydrated, and so water was all he wanted. Now that his throat was no longer chalky, he enjoyed that burning sensation in his chest that only whiskey could ignite.

"Seriously, Robert. You don't look well, and booze before lunch is never a good idea. Maybe today isn't…"

Robert's cell phone rang, drowning out Tab's dialogue.

"Talk," Robert demanded of the caller.

Soon Robert sighed heavily, enough so that the person on the other side of the call could hear him.

"Yeah."

He cleared his throat.

"Hmmph."

He shot Tab a mean look while biting his thumbnail. All of his nails were chewed down, which would later require the services of a trained manicurist.

"Bitch."

He continued to stare at Tab, but his expression changed to something like exasperation.

"Well, fuck you, Belle. Fuck you too. Fuck you very much."

Robert pulled the phone from his ear and mashed the End button with his thumb.

"She did a good job for us," Tab said while looking at the inside of his coffee mug. Then his eyes darted towards Robert for a split second, hoping to gauge his response.

"Belle Hewitt is a pig. Fat old fucking cow."

"Which is she, a pig or a cow?"

"Fuck her and fuck you."

"Listen, Robert. I'm just saying. She kept the show going while you were away. Her ratings were solid. And she picked up on stories where you left off."

"Like The Artist? And Pandro?"

"You were the one that went on national TV and said we needed a whole art school."

"Sure, I was going to slowly take The Artist down a peg or two, in my own way."

"All right."

"On my own schedule, too."

"All right."

"That bitch went off on crazy tangents. Some of that crap she said on the air is just out-and-out nuts."

"But surely last night's news?"

"About Pandro? Yeah, well. I probably need to knock him down a few pegs too. Him and her both. And The Artist too."

"I don't think you're ready to go back on." Once again Tab stared into his coffee mug. There was a hairline crack inside of it.

"Fuck you too, Mister. Let's get out of here and get back to work."

After they returned to the studio, Robert glanced at all the flowers in his main office. He told his secretary to get rid of them.

"Except for the ones you gave me, of course."

"But I…didn't…"

"Well, then, get rid of all of them. I can't stand the sight of them. They're smelling the place up."

The fact was, none of Robert's coworkers sent flowers. Not a single one, not even Tab. All of them were from fans, from people who didn't know him.

During makeup, Robert scanned over his notes before wadding them into a ball and pitching them at a trash can. He missed. By that point, he was psyching himself up for the show.

To give him his due, Tab had done a great job. The set was dressed with a ton of balloons. The rafters were there, exactly as requested, and there wasn't an empty seat. A live studio audience, something that Robert had only rarely used, was cheering his return to the cameras. Fuck Belle Hewitt. This was Robert's show, and these were His people. As the theme music began, a bunch of ticker tape fell from the ceiling. It was like an indoor parade.

"The Robert Lynch Express has just pulled into the station!"

That line really got them going. Robert thought of it himself, off the cuff. When Tab heard him say that, his heart lifted. Maybe everything would return to normal.

Robert tried to calm the opening applause so that he could issue the requisite Thank Yous necessitated by a return to former glory. Then he got down to business.

"As all of you probably know by now, Pandro Burns was picked up by the police last night after shooting a member of the San Francisco city council. He's been charged with murder, which is a pretty strong word to use, I think, given the fact that all he did was take out one of our enemies, and right in their own backyard, right in the middle of the most leftwing cesspool of an American city, but that's neither here nor there, I suppose. Apparently the cops found his fingerprints everywhere. And there is that security footage that showed him firing the gun. And there's something about a ballistics test that proves he did it. So what this means is that his career seems to be at an end, at least temporarily. Maybe a good defense attorney can get him off, but, as all of you know, most trial lawyers are socialists. And we are talking about San Francisco here, people."

That last line caused some titters amongst the assembled slackjaws.

"I hate Ashbury," he said to more giggles.

"Yeah, enough said. But let's not get disheartened, or disgruntled. We are in this together, America. We will overcome. We will have our day. They will rue the day. And we will have our day. Our day will come."

The response was fast and furious. No sign needed to light up and cue this crowd when it was time to applaud. They were true believers.

"I usually don't do this, but I have to relent because all of you Good People are here with me, in my house, so to speak. And I want to be a hospitable host."

With microphone in hand, Robert nodded his head up and down a bit, quickly bit on his lower lip with his upper front teeth, and then made a smack sound. It built a bit of suspense.

"Everyone here today will get an advance copy of my new book, *Letters from the Trenches,* which chronicles my heroic climb back from addiction." He opened his eyes wider, and he used his upper lip to suck on his lower lip. It showed just the tiniest bit of emotion. And it showed resolve.

The crowd applauded.

"The book also has some chapters on a secret drug cartel operating inside the ATF and my thoughts on the evils of modern education."

More applause. Medium shots depicted mothers and daughters, fathers and sons, all clapping and nodding to one another, jointly agreeing that they were fortunate indeed to be seated near Him.

"In order to be a really good host, I want to talk with America. America is in my house today, in the form of all these patriots in the seats in front of me, and I want to hear what America has to say. So, let's get right to it. Any comments or questions?"

No one asked about Robert's drug problem or rehab. Maybe it was because they were getting free books. Maybe it was a show of respect. Or maybe they just didn't care. Everyone's got flaws. They knew that because Robert had told them last time he was on the air.

One man asked about the Middle East; another about India and Pakistan. Two or three more had questions about President Mullins, and Robert had some real zingers ready for them. "President Benedict Mullins Arnold," Robert called him.

Then came a question about The Artist.

"What's your current stand?" a young woman asked.

"You take a stand, dear."

She looked like she didn't know what he meant.

"Stand up, dear, and tell us who you are."

"I'm Amy Kelly, and I'm a sophomore paying my way through NYU." Her voice was nervous, and it cracked as she spoke.

"Good for you, dear. Have you heard what I said college kids should do?"

"You mean about challenging our professors at every lecture, because they can't be trusted?"

"That's it. They're all flaming liberals, and not because they're being burned at the stake, like they should be. What a smart girl, huh, folks? Let's give this young lady a big round of applause."

The audience followed orders while Amy sat back down. She appeared pleased but more than a bit shaken.

"Now, let's get down to business. I've been a supporter, really an ardent admirer of The Artist, at least of his early period. This whole Sportraits business, I mean, come on. Really? I go away for awhile, and it's like the world loses its mind. So, no, I don't approve of his current activities whatsoever. You eliminate political obstacles in order to make the world a better place. You don't murder young kids thanks to some pansy-assed New York law about Kevorkian suicide. And that ridiculous medical degree

The Artist bought from Bolivia? Let me just assure all of you good people that my honorary doctorate is from good ole Liberty University."

Robert swallowed for effect and turned to a different camera.

"Left-wingers."

He shook his head, took a deep breath into his mouth, which he loudly exhaled out of his nose.

"Is The Artist getting preferential treatment in today's society? Well, yes, and I feel responsible for that. Sure. I'll take the blame. Go ahead and sniff. You'll smell burning martyr up here today, folks."

That provoked a few chuckles. Some audience members didn't know whether to laugh or not, mainly because they didn't understand what he meant.

"Now, I'm not saying the worm has turned. The Artist can redeem himself. Everyone deserves a second chance. That's the American way. But he needs to ask for our forgiveness and get his priorities straight. That's what I had to do. In fact, that's what I do do in my new book, *Letters from the Trenches*. Incidentally, it will be be available for Kindle download next week, or, for us graybeards, in hardback at a bookstore near you."

Robert stroked his chin and affected an elderly voice when he said "graybeards." Then, after finishing the book commercial, he raised his left hand to the side of his head and pointed his index finger into the air.

"Pandro has been treated differently than The Artist, who is being shielded from prosecution out there in Jokelahoma, apparently, by idiots who can't seem to find evidence one. But let's face facts. Anyone who gets in on the ground floor of something gets preferential treatment. Law school didn't used to be three years long. Ph.D.'s used to be easier to get. Everyone who forges a certain path makes it harder on those who follow. That's the vicious circle of life."

Robert lowered his head and then slowly moved it from left to right, as if to underscore his exasperation. Then he snapped it back to eye level.

"But no one, and I mean no one, deserves a free lunch. The world doesn't owe us a thing. Let's not forget that. We make our own way. We have to fight for what we get. It isn't about what we *deserve*. It's about struggle. The uphill climb."

Another pause, just the right length. God, he was good. Tab smiled, listening to him finish the show.

"Surely we can't be unfair in our judgments, or unbalanced in our views. We have to tell the truth, to the world, and, most importantly, to ourselves. Wise Up, America! *Wise Up!*"

Tab had asked Robert to glad-hand after the show, to sign some autographs and appear in some quick selfies. Instead, Robert bowed from the waist, waved goodbye, and walked straight out the door.

CHAPTER 26

The Belt Way

"I don't know what to wear," Sadie moaned, half dressed in our hotel room at the Capitol Hill Suites.

I paced up and down the floor.

"Look, Birch," my agent said from the plush chair in the corner. "All I'm saying is that you have to get out there tonight. Smile and shake some hands, you know. That sort of thing."

"Don't you know what they're saying about me in the papers? And on the tube?"

"And the internet," the assistant added, seated uncomfortably at the wooden desk chair.

"Goddammit!" Sadie threw her shoes against the wall.

"You mean that stuff about possible arrest warrants? No. Not a chance. Not if you stay on top. They're still too scared to touch you," the assistant said.

"What we mean is that you *are* untouchable," the agent clarified.

"Look at these fucking heels! I've walked way too far in these," Sadie complained after scooping up her footwear.

"They know I've killed people."

"They know you've *said* that you've killed people. That's it."

"They showed up at the house with a search warrant last week. That's the second time they've searched my pad."

But they've still never found any real evidence," the agent said. "If they did, they'd have already used it."

"I've just got to get the fire back in my belly."

"Joe Cocker wouldn't quit," the agent advised.

Sadie screamed. In fact, she got right in my face, yelling about being too fat and not fitting into her dress and something about her belt size and on and on and on. It was intense.

I said nothing. After all, people were watching.

"Look, the car will be here in a few minutes," the agent said.

"And we've got to grab our flight back to the coast," the assistant added.

Sadie sighed heavily and took a drink from the bottle of gin sitting on the table. She'd been drinking more and more these days. Probably missing her son, too. That's gotta be tough.

When we left the hotel, no one would have known we were upset. Me in my tux, her in the designer dress, with diamonds dripping off her ears, neck, and fingers. When we walked into the Hilton that night, we looked good. Cameras began snapping pix of us and everyone else. The White House Correspondents' Dinner was the biggest of the big. Politicians and stars and celebrities, all in the same room with the President. These were the big guns.

I felt eyes all over me. They belonged to the famous, the infamous, and a healthy dose of unknowns. Together they conveyed every emotion known to man. Anger and hate. Love and admiration. Jealousy and fear. And mostly a bunch of gawking, as if I was some kind of tourist destination like the Grand Canyon.

As we made our way to the WNB table, Lawrence O'Donnell scolded me for avoiding *The Last Word.* David

Frum scowled. P.J. O'Rourke sighed in my general direction, but then smiled. Tricky character, O'Rourke.

Autographs helped. There were only a few requests, but they boosted my confidence. And signing my name gave me something to do with my hands, which were clammy, and it made for a good photo op. These days, I John Hancocked with a paintbrush. It fit the whole Artist image, and it didn't look wussy at all. It really didn't. My agent had assured me of that fact time and again. His assistant agreed.

And they were right about the dinner. It was good to appear to be in command of a situation, and to be part of the In-Crowd. Nowhere was the crowd more important, but ironically no crowd was easier to fit into. Everyone fits in at the press dinner. Here Paula Jones can stand as tall as Brian Williams, who can stand as tall as Angelina Jolie, who can stand as tall, or taller, even, than the President.

Sadie was right in there, yucking it up like she was a star. Her crooked smile ingratiated her to a bunch of celebs. But I understood her well enough to know that she was still pissed at me, her anger percolating just below the surface. Once we got back to the hotel, the volcano would erupt again.

WNB had several tables that night, a testament to their grip on the media, but all of them were located at the back of the room, a testament to their distance from the President and his policies. I was one of their guests, no doubt about it. I wasn't seated next to Robert, or even at his table. That was a snub, but thankfully it went little noticed because Robert was a no-show. He was sick with a previous engagement or something.

For a while, it was tough to hear myself think. The talking heads were all talking. Their collective jabber probably made more sense than what any single one of them was saying, but it was headache fuel all the same.

Once things really got going, the lights dimmed and most people shut up. Not all of them, but most. It was Showtime at the Apollo, with Zeus and the other Olympians in attendance.

Griff Thompson was the featured attraction. I don't really keep up with the new performers much. I prefer the older guys. They might be able to manufacture most things in China, but there are two things ain't nobody making any more of. One is American land. There's only so much of it. The other is Jack Nicholson.

Griff? Well, hell. He was just a two-bit stand-up comedian who got famous two weeks ago, then got a show on Comedy Central last week, and then will probably be getting an unemployment check next week. As for tonight, he was on display, a fixture on the dais right alongside President Mullins. It was hard to see Mullins' face from so far away, but I'll wager that he didn't know who Griff was.

The typical drill is for the idiot onstage to make jabs at the President, and maybe save a few for the Vice-President and other leading politicians. Griff did all that, but then he tore into The Artist.

Unbelievable. Ungoddamnbelievable. I had no choice but to grit my teeth and put on a forced smile for the cameras.

Sadie, who was drunk as all get out, tittered at Griff's line about The Artist's crayons being taken away from him, but after several more of the same, she joylessly stared at the stage. I appreciated her steel, but worried that the press would jump all over the fact she couldn't take a joke.

"So I hear Robert Lynch has asked for a separation from The Artist, right," Griff laughed. "Did you hear this? Did all of you hear this? He finally looked in the mirror and told himself to Wise Up!"

"And, hey, Artist," Griff joked, cupping his hands to his face and looking at me. "Before you go, I've got a get-out-of-jail card for you that I stole from a Monopoly set. You do remember what a monopoly is, don't you? It's what you had until Pandro came to town."

Rat bastard. He wasn't funny, and, besides, he was a real ugly sonbitch. Looked just like a yak.

I wanted to light out for the territories, but the only place I could go was inside of myself. I fantasized about following Griff after the dinner. Screw the back-of-the-side-of-the-head. I started shooting, letting bullets fuck every vital organ. Down, down, down Griff went. Then I shouted "Eat Hickory" and smacked his head with a 2x4. He drooled blood onto the sidewalk while onlookers cheered. Turning around, I spotted President Mullins.

"Birch, I've got a little something for you, Son."

It was a Medal of Freedom, or of Honor, or some such thing. And it sparkled in the moonlight.

Then the President asked for an autograph.

"Put a little doodle next to it, Artist," he joked. "Some kind of drawing or something."

Vultures pecked out Griff's eyes, and Pandro's too. It was my fantasy, so there was nothing wrong with both of them lying there dead, side-by-side.

I was just starting to imagine Robert's head on a pike when Sadie interrupted my chain of thought. It was time to go. Everyone was getting up to leave. The talking heads talked while choking the exits.

"Keep your arm around me, Baby," Sadie told me. "I'm pretty tipsy."

Before we got into the limo, I felt goosebumps enshroud Sadie's skin. I removed my jacket and tried

to put it around her shoulders, but she'd have none of it,
so then we both seemed incomplete. And the air outside was chilly. Damned if the sky wasn't pretty cloudy.
Smelled like rain, a real storm brewing. It was gonna
come a good one.

CHAPTER 27

The Return of the Depressed

"Phone!" Sadie yelled.

I couldn't hear very well when I worked in my office upstairs. It wasn't that big of a home, two stories and maybe 2500 square feet. But it was quite a bit of space for two people. Funny, but we'd hardly been able to enjoy it, always being on the move.

I was surprised that Sadie had gone for the idea of living in Oklahoma, but she did, on the condition she got to choose the new house and decorate the place herself. Most rooms had no furniture.

At my urging, Sadie finally fixed up one of them for her little boy. I still hadn't met him, but I was confident that he'd love his room. Spaceships painted on the walls, with glow-in-the-dark stars glued to the ceiling. A sock monkey sat on the bed with a permanent smile on his face. That's what you call happiness.

Yeah, when things settle down, we'd fly Sadie's mom up from Arkansas and drop Jake off. He was a good boy, Sadie always said. Smart as a whip.

"Phone!"

I peered out of my office, where I was trying to write my memoirs. I hadn't gotten very far. There were lots of notes, and I had filed them meticulously in color-coded folders, each one representing a particular theme or period in my life. All of them fit neatly inside a filing cabinet right beside the desk and my new computer, because you have to have a brand new computer if you're gonna be a writer.

The dedication page was basically finished, but I kept revising it. I couldn't make up my mind whether it should say "To Sadie" or "For Sadie."

Then there was Chapter One. Those two words were all that I had typed. Notes a plenty, written on all manner of scrapnpaper, but no text. Nothing but that little cursor, mocking me each and every time it blinked. Shouting to Sadie gave me a reason to stretch my legs.

"Huh?"

"Phone!"

"Dinner?"

"For God's sake, it's the phone! Get down here!"

I hadn't decided whether or not I liked how bossy Sadie could be. She had so many damned moods. Just as soon as I'd get ready to tell her to shove it, she'd transform into a different person, sweetness and light. Then I'd convince myself that she was perfect. Maybe she did need a boob job, but otherwise she was perfect. Except when she wasn't. Needed Prozac, I figured.

"It's Chet," Sadie whispered, her hand over the receiver.

"Tell him to go to hell."

"He says it's urgent."

I pushed my tongue against the back of my lower teeth as hard as I could and then motioned for the receiver.

"Yeah?"

"I know we haven't been talking much lately," Chet began.

"That was your doing. Or your wife's."

"I just wanted to say that, you know, so, even though I don't agree with some of your decisions recently, well…"

"Well?"

"Well, I think what this woman is doing to you is pretty bad, and I just wanted you to know you've still got people who care about you."

"Woman? What woman? Sadie?"

Overhearing me, Sadie gritted her teeth, braced for attack.

"No, this lady who's going to be on Barry Henderson tonight. They've been running commercials about it all day."

"Who is she?"

"Somebody that's going to talk shit, apparently."

"Shit?" God, I hate that word, even though I used it, parroting my ex-best friend.

"The commercials say something about exposing you."

I pushed my tongue against the back of my teeth again, looked at Sadie briefly, and then went all abrupt.

"Thanks. Uhh…I've gotta go."

I wondered why my agent hadn't phoned, or at least the assistant. As it turned out, they'd frantically been sending emails to Sadie's account, but she hadn't checked it. And they had called and texted repeatedly, but she had the ringer off until moments before Chet phoned. That was because she needed some Quiet Time.

The hours went by slowly until Barry Henderson's program started. After showing a montage of relevant clips, he went right for the jugular. Henderson was a tough journalist, complete with an English accent, but not one of those prissy English accents. It was more like Churchill.

"And you are absolutely sure that this is him?" he asked his guest, showing her a picture of The Artist.

"Yes, yes, that's him. It was one of the most unforgettable nights of my life. I'll never forget his face."

I hadn't forgotten her face either. I never knew her name, but she was my first victim. The gal that got away. Needless to say, I didn't keep a file full of notes about her.

"So, Fran, tell us what happened, what really happened that night."

Fran. Bitch's name was fucking Fran, I thought, unaware at that moment of how profanity was increasingly populating my mind.

"It was scary, so scary," Fran said. "It was all so very scary."

She didn't look frightened at all. Cheap turbo blonde with dark eyes encircled by black makeup. Leather jacket with zippers everywhere on it. I wondered whether people actually keep stuff in the pockets behind all those zippers, or if the zippers were just there for looks.

"What actually happened between you two?" Henderson probed.

"I was walking along. I was in college back then, very young and innocent. And I was walking along, in the dark of night, and I took a short cut behind this old building, and there he was." Her voice changed to a whimper, kind of a like a bad actress in a B-movie.

"The Artist."

"Yeah, but he didn't call himself that then."

"What did he call himself?"

"I don't know. He didn't say."

"So he might have called himself The Artist, and you wouldn't have known?"

"I guess so."

"You didn't ask his name?"

"Oh no, I was too scared. It was all very scary."

"Right. And then?"

"Then he pulled a gun on me. In fact, he had a knife in one hand and a gun in the other."

"What happened next?"

"Well, he pointed the gun at me."

"What happened to the knife he was holding?"

"I don't know. Maybe he put it back in his pocket. Or maybe he dropped it. Yeah, he dropped it. But he definitely pointed the gun at me, and I was frightened."

"And?"

"And he looked me right in the eyes, and he screamed, 'You've been offed!' Then he looked away, like he couldn't bear to watch. And he tried to squeeze the trigger, but he couldn't."

"He couldn't pull the trigger?" Henderson snickered. Actually, it was less a snicker than a guffaw.

"Well, no. That's why I'm alive here to tell the tale, I guess. He dropped the gun and ran off."

"What did you do then?"

"I just stood there for awhile, and when I was sure he was gone, and it wasn't some kind of strange act, you know, to trick me, I picked up that gun and put it in my purse, you know, for protection."

"Did you not consider picking up his knife as well?"

"I guess not. Maybe he didn't drop it after all."

"And you've got the very same gun for sale on eBay right now?"

"It's being auctioned. I think it has about four days left, and I just want everyone to know that I'm giving ten percent of the proceeds to my church."

"Isn't that odd?"

"Well, no. That's what you call a tithe. You see, I'm a churchgoing lady. I was born again a few years ago."

"Now, just to be clear, you did report this incident to the police?"

"Yes, it's all in the original police report, except the part about me keeping his gun. But everything else is down in black-and-white."

"What else do you remember about The Artist?"

"I guess he was sort of sexy, you know, in a dumb sort of way. But now, I never thought he'd become famous, you know, like on TV and everything."

"Maybe you should have given him your phone number. He's probably worth a good deal of money these days." Henderson was trying to be funny, but in my book he sounded snide.

"I really don't think that's appropriate talk."

"May I ask what your politics are?"

"I really don't see what that has to do with anything."

"Of course it does. If you are a liberal, you might just be making this stuff up to damage the reputation of a man who is, or certainly was, a conservative icon."

"We're not supposed to be talking about stuff like that."

"I decide that. I'm the host, and it is a relevant question. Really, Fran, I've read that police report and there's nothing in it that definitively links your would-be murderer to The Artist. Plus, it was very dark that night. You've said so yourself."

"This is not what I agreed to talk about."

Henderson repeated his question, but by that point Fran probably couldn't hear him. She yanked the clip-on microphone from her leather jacket, stood up from her chair, and bumbled off the set. The interview was over.

Sadie lifted the remote and turned the TV off. She tilted her head and gave me a skeptical look.

"Is it true?"

"No…no. Absolutely not. I did not have a knife with me that day. That hussy's just making that part up. Totally making it up. I know it looks bad, but, well…out of this wreckage I will arise."

"Stop quoting Asia," she said derisively.

Then both of us fell silent, staring not at each other, but at the darkened television screen.

CHAPTER 28

Kingmaker

"Where the hell are you? I know you're in here," Tab said after opening the door to Robert's dark office.

Robert sat behind his desk with his legs crossed, and said nothing. He was too busy scribbling notes on a yellow legal pad. Tab turned on the lights and opened the blinds. He spied an open bottle of Jack Daniels on the floor right in front of Robert.

"How much did you drink?"

"I wish I could say I killed it, but even now it lives." Robert didn't bother looking up at his companion.

"You look terrible. Let's get you some coffee and makeup."

Tab leaned against the desk and looked out the window. Another rainy day, but he knew that everything appears more colorful in the rain. He remembered that from his old photography class. Sunny days might feel happier, but cloudy days cause everything to look nicer. When buildings and grass and everything else don't have to reflect the sun's rays, their colors actually appear more vibrant. Tab's glass was temporarily half full.

Robert kept scribbling, but then he spoke again.

"Not just yet. I'm nearly finished organizing my thoughts."

"You going to use it?"

"Of course I am. Why not? I should never have bothered playing kingmaker," he chuckled. "I'm the king."

"So does that make me the court jester?"

"No, you're the queen." Robert laughed.

"Seriously."

"Yeah, I've got him in my sights, and now I'm going to pull the trigger."

"Is that…"

"Wise? Well…Wise Up, America!"

Tab exhaled loudly.

"You see, Tab, when I was a little kid, the art teacher liked *my* drawings. She told me that I was really talented, but she didn't say that to the dumbass kid sitting next to me."

"Is that true, or did you steal that story from The Artist?"

"His story *is* my story."

"Robert."

"Tab?" Robert said, lowering his voice mockingly.

"Birch was good for ratings, but…"

"But don't you get it. He's not a true believer. Not like WNB. Not like us. Not like you and me."

"Weren't you a Liberal until 1988?"

"So?"

"You supported Dukakis, right?"

"That's different, man. I wasn't a true believer then. But I am now. I wised up." He chortled.

"Will you at least finish your notes while you're in makeup?"

After having been back on the air for a few weeks, Robert ditched the live audience. Sometimes it served a purpose. But every once in awhile, frenemies invaded the ranks and grilled him with tough questions.

So Robert went back to an old routine that he hadn't used in quite awhile. The studio lights were dimmed so that his Power Point slides were visible oncamera. Off to the side, standing at a podium, Robert wore reading glasses low on his nose and held a laser pointer. It gave him the appearance of being a teacher, or university professor even. The appearance of knowing What's What.

The result was compellingly boring TV. And today's lecture was about The Artist's downfall.

"Now, about Fran Applebie," Robert said to camera two. "Is she telling the truth? That's the question people are asking. Which is really a question about The Artist. Was he a pansy that day when he couldn't pull the trigger? A little wimp? An impotent little freak that tried to shoot a helpless young lady and failed? I don't know. Maybe. Probably. She does have the smoking gun."

Robert grinned devilishly.

"Of course, I should really say the non-smoking gun, shouldn't I?"

Then Robert winked at everyone and no one.

"Now, I could have gotten Fran on here as a guest, but you know, America, I hate to waste your time with guests when you can have wall-to-wall me. Let's just say, for the sake of argument, that Fran is telling the truth. It would really fit a pattern, wouldn't it? I mean, let me just say one word to you."

Robert licked his lips and then cleared his throat for dramatic effect.

"Sportraits."

When he spoke that word, Robert affected an effeminate voice and made air quotes right next to his cheeks.

"Sportraits represents the taking of innocent lives, which is something I know that I personally could never, ever condone. Shameful. Completely and utterly shameful. It is murder, whatever the dangerous secular progressives here in New York say about doctor-assisted suicide."

Robert looked down reverentially, then lifted his head.

"But that's not the end of the story, is it? You see, our producers have obtained some cell phone footage taken backstage at a Sportraits event a few months ago. This comes at no little expense, because the person who filmed it was originally going to sell it to TMZ. And I really believe, America, that you will be shocked. And appalled. Shocked and appalled. Roll tape."

The footage was shaky, but it showed Birch and Sadie chatting with some fans. At one point, while signing an autograph for a huge, linebacker-type Neanderthal, Birch seemed to say, "Well, women. Most of them belong in whorehouses or mental institutes. Goddamned cages, even." But then again, it might have been dubbed, because the lips and words seemed out-of-sync and the voice didn't sound quite like Birch. There were also a few suspicious edits.

Robert replayed that line three or four times and used his laser pointer to draw circles around Birch's mouth, as if that would help make the bad audio easier to hear. WNB subtitles also spelled the words for the audience.

"He's a blasphemer, ladies and gentlemen. He's irreverent, and he's also a misogynist. Speaking as an unabashed supporter of women everywhere, particularly all those housewives out there in TV land, you know, this strikes at everything I view as holy."

Robert looked back up at the footage, which he had intentionally paused at an odd moment. The freeze frame captured Birch with an expression on his face that made him look like he was about to gag.

"What can I say, America? I've been disappointed so many times from the people I look up to, but this…this is an insult to everything I believe in. A slap in the face. I mean who exactly can you trust anymore?"

Then he stuck his index finger up to his ear, as if he was straining to hear something on a little headphone.

"What's this? What's this? We've got some breaking news coming through for you, America."

Robert really didn't have breaking news. He was just putting a good spin on something that he'd already known for over an hour.

"Our friend Pandro has released a formal statement. All of you know Pandro, I'm sure. Our thoughts and prayers are with him, incidentally. And on our website at WNB Dot Com Slash Wise Up America!, which does in fact end with an exclamation point, you can make a donation to his legal fund. Well, Pandro is now under house arrest pending trial, and he has released a statement. It reads as follows."

Robert pulled a piece of paper out of his breast pocket.

"Originally The Artist was my hero, my inspiration, my muse. But as it turns out, he is just a fraud. If you stop and look at it, he's been given a free ride for what amounts to taking out only three of America's enemies. What's he done for us lately? In fact, what's he ever really done for us? At the end of the day, he's an embarrassment, which is all-too-clear thanks to these latest revelations."

Robert folded the paper carefully, and returned it to his breast pocket with special care, as if it was a precious historical document worthy of preservation.

"Pandro arrests my case. Let's all wise up, America. Each dog has his day, but at the end of that day, a dog, well…a dog is still a dog."

After smiling briefly at that line, he stared into the camera for a moment, pursing his lips before signing off.

"From New York, America. That's our show."

CHAPTER 29

Wishing

I've always thought it was strange the way some old churches in big cities go out of business and later the vacant buildings turn into things like nightclubs. And then you have a country checkered with old Wal-Marts that get closed down when bigger and better Wal-Marts open just up the street. A few of them have turned into mega-churches, or at least small churches with loads of extra space inside. And a long walk from the pulpit to the restroom, probably.

How does a church go out of business? What's its last day of business like? Hard to tell. Probably varies depending on the time and place.

But the junk about nightclubs and Wal-Marts was stranger. Or at least it stopped and made you think. Is there an expiration date on how long specific locations remain sacred?

That played on my mind in the days following Sadie's suicide.

I found her in the garage, the car still running. Carbon monoxide had always frightened me when I heard about it as a kid. The silent killer. The odorless killer. Once upon a time, it had been spooky. Now it just seemed greedy.

After making sure she was dead, I turned off the engine, opened the garage door, and called 9-11. I thought about crying, but elected not to. The press was already harping on me for being a wuss. That kind of thing had destroyed

Muskie. Sure, a few politicians, like Boehner, have turned on the waterworks hardcore in recent years, but deep down even their supporters have to cringe at that crap.

To keep my mind occupied, I gazed upon all the boxes in the garage. One after the other, stacked vertically. They were different sizes, so the stacks were haphazard. God only knows what was in them. A lot of it was Sadie's. Things shipped from her Chicago apartment that she'd probably half-forgotten about it. Things I had never even seen, things I never knew existed, if they did at all.

I was pretty numb from the shock. I couldn't feel my cheeks, and Sadie's were cold. People say corpses look like they're sleeping, but that wasn't true, not with Sadie anyhow. No breathing, no snoring, no rapid eye movement. She was just dead. The smile had left her eyes.

The brigade of photographers camped out in front of the house didn't bother me. Par for the course. The whole thing seemed like a bad dream that washes away in the shower. Except it wasn't washing away.

The cops found a note in her jean pocket. Short and sweet. In all caps, it said:

"BABY, I LOVE YOU DEARLY. PLEASE TAKE
CARE OF YOURSELF, AND PLEASE, PLEASE
TAKE CARE OF JAKE. GOODBYE, SADIE MAY."

Sadie May. She always said that was what her mother called her when she was in trouble. Sadie May, with a heavy accent on the middle name. In response, I used to tease that her middle name should have been stronger, more definitive, like "Sadie Will."

As for taking her own life, I thought and thought and thought some more. Should I have known? Could I have done this or that? We had played some crazy sex games where I'd pretend to kill her, holding a gun to the back-of-the-side-of-her-head. One time she even put the tip of it in her mouth. But that was all in good fun. It never seemed like she really meant it when she asked me to shoot her.

And everything else, well, I couldn't say. It wasn't like in the movies where you had clear cause-and-effect, or a detective novel where some Frenchie with a waxed moustache easily reconstructs all the things that led up to the big event. Maybe the Mystery of Sadie's Crooked Smile couldn't be solved.

Maybe *that* was the solution, the fact that I would never know. The solution was that there was no solution. I had never heard Sadie say anything suicidal, but come to think of it, she hadn't said much of anything for a few weeks. The sex had gone dry. And we were sleeping in separate bedrooms, mainly because she snored all the time. I did too, I guess.

When she was awake, she'd get mad and scream a lot, and then calm down and act like the day when I met her, and then later she'd scream some more. I didn't know whether she was happy or sad or what. To be honest, she didn't seem any different than she ever had. I guess there were signs, but if there were, I sure didn't see them. And it's hard to remember something you never knew.

The first few nights, I couldn't sleep at all. I shifted from room to room, most of which were still completely empty. Empty except for the new carpet and those little balls of fuzz that collect on top of it. Then I moved into Jake's room. Tears welled in my eyes when I stared up at the glow-in-the-dark stars on the ceiling. Then I cried and cried.

Part of the problem was television. It used to be that, if you couldn't sleep, you could turn on the TV in the middle of the night and there would be snow. The white noise was clean and consistent and comforting. And if you had to open your eyes, sometimes you could see images form in the festering fuzz. Years ago, long before I had any interest in politics, I saw a faint vision of Richard Nixon in all that snow, more than once. I never knew if it was my imagination, or maybe just a weak signal from a station that was beyond the reach of my antennae.

None of that mattered now. If you turn on the TV, you have constant programming on hundreds of channels. I used to ponder the meaning of the word "forever," but now I get it. Modern TV has no ending. It's 24/7, or 25/8, as Chet used to say, laughing.

The second morning without Sadie found me bleary-eyed and achy, particularly between my shoulder blades. I could feel my bones. Along with the Prozac, I shoveled some Valium into my mouth. I wanted to take out the trash, but the press was still parked on the front lawn, so I had to make do with piling it up in the garage.

All of the Cocker tapes went. Sadie hated his music, and so now I did too. Maybe throwing out stuff would help my soul, or my head, or at least my digestion.

Of course I kept the Asia albums, because they were too good not to keep. And I reshelved my JFK library inside the den. Sadie would approve. She once admitted that it was history, and you can't get rid of history, even if you do stick it in the attic for awhile.

Within a few days, my agent's assistant arranged for a car to pick me up and head to the airport. Sadie's body had already been shipped to Montana for the funeral. Now it was time to follow her there. Flashes went off as I approached the limo, but they weren't strong enough to brighten my eyes, which were hidden behind some dark shades.

On the way to the airport, I unholstered my cell phone and played with the ring tones just to have something to do. I saw the number of backlogged text messages that I had never bothered reading. Among them was one from Sadie that made no immediate sense. It said ">3."

Huh.

Montana was my second choice, Europe being the first. But you have a limited time frame when it comes to corpses, and there were just too many visa problems when it came to burying Sadie in Europe, which she had always dreamed of visiting. And of course we used to talk about taking a trip to Phuket. That name made her giggle, at least the way she pronounced it, but it was just a joke. So I settled on Montana, which was one of the many states that she had never visited. Sadie always wanted to travel, and so this trip became my final gift to her.

I spared no expense: a horsedrawn hearse, no easy thing to find in the new millennium, and a beaut of a casket. Plus a vault, because you have to buy a vault if you have any sense at all. It keeps the moisture and the worms out. You can't cheap out on the big sleep. If you do, you're just a fucker, that's all.

At the funeral home, I tucked Sadie's pet rock Cherry into her pocket. Then I whispered "Ulalume" into her ear, but I didn't know why.

Somehow the paparazzi found the cemetery and kept taking pictures the whole time, but I didn't care. I wore my sunglasses, as well as a black suit and tie. My agent and my agent's assistant and my publicist were there, all dressed in black. They held black umbrellas too, even though it wasn't raining. It was the least they could do.

Sadie's mother was nowhere to be found, but that was cool. Some people can't stomach death, and she did have to look after Jake. It was just as well that the kid didn't have to watch his momma go into the ground. I sure didn't want anybody to see me that way, which was I was going to be cremated and released into the air, a kind of darker version of white noise.

When the preacher finished, my publicist held up a boom box. It was an old one, but it still worked great. Lots of bass, and it had that great dual cassette feature for making copies. Right on cue, she hit the play button, which made a nice chunk sound when it was depressed.

After a couple seconds of hiss, Asia's old song *Wishing* filled the air. It was a perfect tune. It should have been a hit, but it wasn't.

CHAPTER 30

Mending Fences

Chet was late.

I arrived early and ducked into a little table at the back of the golf course clubhouse. The newspaper-in-front-of-the-face trick helped, but not as well as it used to. Newspaper pages have gotten so much littler in recent years. It used to be that you had to open them up and crease the pages in the opposite direction just to read an article inside, that's how big they were. Now newspapers are small.

It was good to be back at the course, even though we probably wouldn't do any golfing. Since making it big, I had hardly played golf at all, except for a junket to Pennsylvania with that Super PAC guy. Good trip, but it was only four days and Sadie was too sick to go. "Next time," she had promised that morning, hiding her head under the pillow.

I hadn't seen Chet face-to-face for months, and I was still kind of irritated at him, but after the Fran thing and Sadie's death, all that was in the past. I thought about that word, "past," and how much it sounded like the word "passed," and how maybe the two words were practically the same.

If it had been a woman who was running this late, I would have been worried about getting stood up, but not with Chet. Chet always ran late. That was his way of doing things. His m.o. He'd turn up. It was just a question of when.

My eyes rolled over the newspaper page, but I didn't read the words. I was deliberating on how to play our reunion. Act tough at first, or maybe pretend nothing had ever happened? It was hard to tell, but suddenly there was no more time to think about it. The top of my newspaper crumpled downward in Chet's hand.

"Hey!"

"Get caught in traffic?"

"Not really." Chet smiled and then sat down. "Hit a lot of red lights, but it's all good. I downloaded some Alan Parsons Project the other day, and finally got to hear some of it. *Eye in the Sky* and some of the Poe stuff."

"Cool," I said with a tiny smile.

"Somebody told me the other day that Parsons was just a producer and stuck his name on the band."

"Urban legend. Parsons was a producer and an engineer, but he really did co-write those songs. And he played keyboard and stuff."

"Same guy also told me that *Dark Side of the Moon* sells so many copies that somewhere in Germany or Europe or someplace there's a factory that spends all day burning copies of nothing but that one album. You think that's true?"

"Never cared for Pink Floyd. Say, can you move your chair a bit to the right?"

"Your right or mine?"

"Yours."

"Why?"

"You're blocking my view of the entrance."

"And?" Chet said.

"I need to keep an eye on things."

"Why don't we just trade places?"

"I can't have my back to the door."

"Worried?"

I glanced around, deciding not to answer because the waitress was bouncing up to our table.

"Excuse me, sir. Can I get you anything to drink?"

"Club soda."

"And you sir? Another mint julep?"

"Still working on this one."

She walked away, unimpressed.

"Your agent said you were working on your memoirs?"

"Yup."

"How's that going?"

"Not so good. Maybe it's too soon."

"I don't know. A lot's happened."

I nodded, and then slurped the last of my drink. I had wanted to order a cocktail with fruit in it, but thought that might look wussy. Mint was a middle-ground option.

"They do say everyone has a book in them."

"Yeah, well. The problem is that everybody only has one book in them, and it's a book that's been written before."

"Your's hasn't."

I raised my eyebrows as if they were question marks. After an uncomfortable pause, I changed the subject, asking Chet if he thought the authorities were finally going to arrest me.

"Tough to say. Maybe. If your TV pal keeps throwing you under the bus, yeah, probably. If they can dig up evidence. They must not have anything more than your own statements to the press."

"What if they find something?"

"We're in Oklahoma. What do you think?"

I didn't respond, but clenched my glass and shook it a bit. It was at the point where the melting ice and the last of my drink had almost turned into water.

"After Sadie, you know, what more is there? Seems like it's time to pack it in."

"Hey, don't give up now. That's just what they want you to do."

"Great minds don't think alike."

"I'm being serious."

"But you were more down on me than anybody."

"Well, we all change, even though sometimes it comes slow."

"So, what, you're a conservative now?"

"No…I was actually thinking more about you."

"What do you mean?"

"Reinvent yourself. Get popular again. That'll show 'em."

Then a cell phone began to ring. I looked at Chet, who shook his head to indicate he didn't recognize the sound. My own phone was on the table, next to my glass. It was silent.

"Your coat," Chet suggested.

My left hand patted one pocket on my sports jacket. It was empty. Then I tried another pocket and felt a foreign object. I lifted it into the light. Sadie's phone. I had wanted it nearby just to keep a tiny piece of her with me.

Scrutinizing the number, I saw the 479 area code. Sadie's mom.

"Hello, is this Birch?"

"Yes. Yes it is."

"Honey, I'm so glad you picked up. I never had your own number, but I just wanted to thank you for taking care of the funeral arrangements. I wish Sadie had been buried here in Arkansas, but she's at peace now, and that's all that matters."

"Yeah, well, it's so nice to finally talk to you. I always hated that you couldn't make it to the wedding."

"Sadie didn't tell me about it until it was over. But I surely do appreciate all the money you've sent."

"Well, as long as I can, I'll keep it up. I'm sure it'll help with Jake's college fund."

"What's that, darlin'?"

"Jake."

"Jake?"

"Your grandson."

"My grandson?"

"Sadie told me so much about him."

"Sadie?"

"Your daughter?"

"I know who Sadie is, darlin'."

"Is Jake some kind of nickname?"

"For who?"

"For Sadie's little boy."

"There's got to be some kind of mistake. Sadie never had any children."

"Oh…oh. Yeah, well. Yeah. Okay."

"Thanks again for all the money."

I turned Sadie's phone off without saying goodbye and shoved it back into my coat pocket.

"Everything okay there, hoss?"

"Yeah…sure."

"Listen, I better get back to the office. But do me a solid and think about what I told you."

CHAPTER 31

This Is a Recording

"I don't chew my cabbage twice."

Grrblipppdepipp.

"chew my cabbage twice."

After rewinding the tape some more, I clicked the STOP button. There were hours of this rabble, enough so that I needed to buck up and hire a secretary to transcribe all of it. Usually I tune out other people; now I was tuning myself out.

To be honest, I blamed my new psychiatrist, Susan, though granted I only see her rarely, because at 105 dollars an hour, there's not that much worth talking about. Her rate is supposed to be cheap, at least by comparison, but it never feels cheap, and sometimes I really worry about that $5. How does one arrive at that kind of figure, unless the fiver covers the office electric bill, and the C-note is pure profit?

I like the fact Susan is a woman, except when I don't. She suggested that I keep a journal, especially since my appointments with her are irregular. Plus she claims my depression triggers memory loss. I'm not sure about that, though, because I never seem to forget the bad stuff.

Generally the thought of doing paperwork horrifies me, even though I prefer the thought of real paperwork over whatever word will necessarily replace it, given that fewer people use real paper in today's world. The damnable tide. Makes me want to order a new rolodex or buy a used mimeograph machine just to show 'em.

I jabbered such random concepts into my microcassette recorder. On a particular setting, I can record an hour of tape per side. Plus, I can push the REW and FF buttons while the tape is still playing, to scan for important thoughts I want to hear again.

Vzhubugurbabugurba.

"My urine looks pretty cloudy these days."

Wuzhhhopnubuff. Yzzrrupbuflurphah.

"Another crock of crap."

Bfurbugleepbleepgleepzhuhuzzuz.

"And why isn't the word 'masculinist' a word? There's 'feminist,' so why not 'masculinist?' I mean, why do men's colognes these days smell like sweet perfume, like they belong in atomizers, even though the word 'atomizers' could sound more masculine, and would sound more masculine, if people would think of nuclear power when they say it."

Undulatazoopzipnum. Merkverktooblap.

"I'm curtailed in the modern world, something awful. At times, I want to just kill some people, not like anything to do with advancing my career, but just when some folks get out of line and need to be taught a lesson, that's the time to smash them. But I can't do that, you know, because it would be all like, Birch is a bad guy, even though the other person started it."

Zhup. Zhububupupp.

"Curtailed is exactly the word that I was going for. My natural impulses as a man and as a human being are completely curtailed by the niceties of today's world. I mean, I want to be nice. There's a bit of hard bark on me, sure, but I want to be nice. No one on God's green earth could dispute that. But it feels like I have to put up with a lot of garbage that belongs in other people's trashcans."

Vrrupvrequasadulabutubuprrrrrrzivifivichitich.

"And so this hag is a guest in our kindergarten class for some reason or other, I don't know, and she proceeds to talk about how Santa isn't real, but just like something we *used* to believe in. But I was just four or five. Hell, I believed in him. I still do, sort of."

I stopped the tape because something was rustling in my ear. It was a few hairs growing in the canal. I could feel them, several of them, so I used my thumb and forefinger to pluck them out, one by one. Little tears came into my eyes, but nothing could be done about it. My personal hair trimmer didn't work anymore.

Gluptihubbrefindalepookluhfrunundoll.

"Subpar. The *Weekly Standard* called me subpar."

As the tape kept playing, I stared into the mirror, fearful that my hairline might be receding a bit. Surely I wouldn't go bald, not even as an old man. I'll always need my hair.

Arippadippurnikkkanicktikkagenu.

"And so, uhh, what was I fixing to talk about? Oh yeah. Love. Some idiot in college told me that love and hate aren't very different from one another. I think he said that in a philosophy class. Now, there's a bunch of nonsense if there ever was. Love is love and, as far as hate goes, a guy needs enemies. Enemies keep the order of things."

"I suppose there are some occasional gray areas. Like, in the game Dungeons & Dragons, black pudding is a monster that you fight. In Ireland, black pudding is a breakfast food that you eat. But then, maybe that's a difference without a distinction."

I ejected that tape and inserted another, though I don't know why I bothered. For lack of anything better to do, I clicked PLAY.

Hisssssssssssssssssssssssssssssss.

"Tape nine starts now. Yes, now. We're on. Uhhh. Let's see. Yeah. *Uhhhhhhhhhooooohhhhhyeaahhhh.* I was thinking in the shower this morning that fame may not really be the most important thing, that maybe it's time I get involved in charitable work, you know, because at heart I do want to make the world a better place for all of us."

Tubburbichlippivicarovnonichka.

"The words 'resemble' and 'reassemble' are so similar. There's got to be a reason why."

Quertaxzibulippityblip.

"But back to what I was really aiming to get at, maybe I *should* be a preacher, you know, someone who could inspire people and comfort them because, I mean, it is a fact that Charles Guiteau was a preacher. 'Course he was a preacher before he shot President Garfield, but my order of events could make more sense chronologically, like in terms of repentance or evolution."

Funnnnnuptiburpalot.

CHAPTER 32

Regurgitations

"And from New York, America...That's our show."

As Robert ended the program, he gripped some papers in his hands. Nothing was written on them. They were just a prop. He liked to hold them up vertically and tap them on top of the table, straightening them into a stack as if they were a big deck of cards.

When a summer intern nervously approached him, Robert prepared to deal one of the blank pages in front of her, something he could autograph. Interns were always too broke to buy his books.

She looked quizzically at the pen in his hand before speaking.

"Tab said he needs to see you."

"Tab?"

"Yes. I mean, yes sir. In his office."

"In *his* office?"

"His office. Yes...yes sir."

It was Robert's turn to look quizzical. He marched off the set, down the corridor, up the elevator, down another corridor, down another corridor, and then down another corridor. His slippers shuffled the whole way, which hardly helped his bunions.

By the time he reached Tab's office, Robert was incensed. They were supposed to meet in Robert's office or at the coffee shop. That was the deal.

Robert took a deep breath and kicked the door open. Not that hard, but hard enough to open it, and hard enough to let Tab hear his displeasure. In the process, Robert's right slipper flew off his foot.

Tab's lights were off and the curtains were drawn. The room's only illumination came from a group of candles sitting on a table between two sofas in the corner of the room. Robert was still angry, but had to transfer most of his energy into squinting.

"What the fuck are all these candles?"

"I've used them for months," Tab said. "You just never come to my office anymore."

"Anymore?" Robert asked with the arrogance of a spoiled brat.

"They're therapeutic."

"Sounds gay to me."

"Well, they put off a nice scent."

"They're covering up a bad smell, you mean."

"So?"

"Yeah."

"I talked to the big man."

"The big man?"

"You know who I am mean, Robert."

"Mr. Nance, I presume?"

"Bigger."

"Bentley?"

"Yeah."

"Well, what did you talk to him about?"

"He owns the fucking place, Robert. He talked to me."

"And?"

"He put it all in this memo."

Robert grabbed the single page out of Tab's hand. Without reading it, he noticed the initials TB. Tom Bentley, WNB's owner. Normally station manager Carter

Nance relayed important news, but this time Bentley directly spoke from on high, even if from his office in England, where he kept a tight grip on his united media kingdom.

Robert wadded the memo into a ball and held it over one of the candles. As it started to burn, he looked in vain for an ashtray.

"No one smokes around here anymore, Robert."

Robert puffed out some air to extinguish the small flame and then held the charred paper between his thumb and index finger. He stared at the red edges, which were turning ashen gray when he spoke again.

"So what did he want?"

"This whole Free Pandro campaign. Bentley wants it to stop. Now."

"Why?"

"He says the thing with The Artist worked, but it was a one-of-a-kind thing, and now it's time to move on. Lots of folks are unhappy."

"Our ratings are up."

"Not anymore."

"Well, they shot up after I first discovered The Artist."

"They sure did, but that's in the past. Everyone's used to all of this now."

"So?"

"Bentley was clear."

"But that's me. That's my thing."

"It's over, Robert. Just drop the Pandro garbage and go back to beating up on the President. That's perfect for you. The election is only a year away. You can really make a difference."

"Fuck this. Lots of networks would die to get me," Robert said half-heartedly, knowing it wasn't true.

"Yeah, well."

"I'll start my own fucking station. Oprah did it."

"You don't have Oprah's numbers."

"Close."

"Oprah didn't even have Oprah's numbers."

"I'm not going softly into that dark night." Robert started to point to the outside world, but with the lights off he could hardly make out where the windows were.

"No one's asking you to go. Just tone it down. And get back on the President. Back on message. That's where the money is."

"I could start my own website."

"You have a website."

"I mean with webcasts and shit."

"Your site is regularly updated with unique footage."

"No, no, I'm saying that that would be it. We could run our own show and put it online and charge for subscriptions and shit."

"Robert, please. Just take it easy. You know, since the rehab you've been really, you know…Just take it easy. Get a good night's rest, and we'll have coffee in the morning."

"Don't ask me to come to your office again. Ever."

Robert didn't say anything else. He silently got on all fours, moving his hands across the carpet until he discovered the missing slipper. Then he left the room and made the winding journey back to his own office. He needed to grab his suit jacket, he reminded himself. The sweat on the armpits of his white shirt had dried, but it left ugly dark spots.

When he reached his destination, Robert closed the door quietly behind him and practically leapt for the filing cabinet. Therein was a new bottle of Jack Daniels, and the cap made a great sound as each of its little umbilical cords tore off the plastic ring.

Robert held the bottle with both hands and lifted it to his lips, guzzling the whiskey as fast as he could. Some of it escaped out of his bottom lip, running down his chin and onto his shirt but, what the hell. It was already discolored. He didn't care about his clothes, or about the blank pages on his desk that were soaking up the spillover. He held his two hands higher and higher to suck down as much of the booze as he could.

Some of it backed into his nose, which caused him to slam the bottle down onto his desk. He could hear that it knocked something over, and when he opened his eyes he saw that it was a picture frame. Not the one of his kids or the one of his parents. It was the photo of Roger Mudd.

Robert had never met Mudd, but he had always admired him, particularly as a kid. Mudd was old school. A great TV journalist and anchor at CBS and NBC. One of the all-time champs. Robert had always told everyone that Mudd was the reason he got into the game. And it was true.

Picking the photo up, Robert noticed it was really dusty. Some secretary or maid or somebody should have cleaned this, he thought to himself as he tried to stare through the dirt. He hadn't even realized he was crying until a couple of the teardrops fell quietly onto glass frame, mixing with the grime rather than cleaning it.

Robert carefully sat the photo back onto his desk and rubbed his eyes. He spotted his jacket hanging on the back of his office door and walked towards it. When he did, he stumbled and hit one of his knees on something. Too much booze. After a few seconds, he stood up and made it to the door.

Time to go, he thought, staggering towards the elevator. He pushed the down button over and over again.

The pain he felt in his knee seemed to be getting worse. He'd really messed it up. And he'd forgotten to replace his slippers with shoes.

Once Robert was inside, the two metal doors shut and the elevator jerked downwards. He saw the digital numbers go from ten to nine to eight to seven. It was like the countdown before a rocket launch.

But then everything stopped. Takeoff was aborted. Robert fumbled at the buttons, but nothing happened. The fucking elevator was stuck. He grabbed for his phone, but it wasn't in his pocket. He'd left it in his office with his shoes. So he pushed the emergency button.

His knee throbbed and his head started to heat up. That was when he got that green feeling in his tummy. Breakfast, lunch, coffee, booze. All of it spewed violently onto the elevator floor.

Robert had to rest. It was like the whole world was sitting on top of his drunken shoulders, so he squatted down to the side of his vomit. The rancid odor caused him to throw up again. Sweat poured off his brow and armpits. He felt green again, but the third time unleashed little more than a succession of dry heaves and an amazingly horrible taste in his mouth.

He untucked and unbuttoned his shirt, hoping to cool down. And then he sat and he sat and he sat.

After ten or fifteen minutes, more or less, he grabbed onto the railing and stood up just long enough to hit the emergency button again. This time it made a buzzing sound. Fuck! Fuck, fuck, fuckety fucking fuck! The first time he must not have actually pushed it hard enough.

Once again Robert slumped onto the floor, still feeling hot and wildly out of breath. But more than anything else, he was hungry, like his body was completely empty. It came over him like a tidal wave. A crazy appetite, as if he was starving. He hadn't eaten dinner, and he'd lost breakfast and lunch. In fact, to be perfectly honest, he hadn't eaten any breakfast and lunch had been fairly small. And now he was so fucking hungry, hungrier than he had ever been in his entire life, as if his body was totally empty.

It took another five or ten minutes before the elevator finally started moving. By that time, all of the vomit was gone. And even though Robert had just eaten, he was still hungry.

CHAPTER 33

The Artist 2.0

Nowadays, automated phone systems and ATMs are more polite than people. They say "Please" and "Thank You." I'm generally down on emergent technology, but I do respect respect, and that's what you get from machines.

My mind tried to process that contradiction as I inspected my house. The empty rooms were now full, and the full rooms were now empty. It was my new headquarters. The big HQ. And the whole team was there, except for my agent and my agent's assistant. They dumped me immediately after I announced my plan. My Grand Design. Chet was a fool, they had argued till they were out of breath, but it really wasn't Chet's plan. Chet had just pointed me in the right direction. Reinvent yourself. Get popular again.

Now the publicist, the one who had always been so quiet, was running the show. Grace. That's her name. Sadie probably knew it, but I had never even bothered. Anyhow, in order to Make Things Happen, Grace had hired an attorney, two writers, a graphic artist, a filmmaker, a sculptor, and a slew of internet gurus. It cost a pretty penny. Presumably. I left all that to my accountant.

The whole gang was friendly, except the sculptor, who kept his distance. All the rest of them stopped what they were doing when they spotted me, saying hello and so forth. It did my heart good, really, to see that everything was changing.

"What do you think of the T-Shirt prototype?" Grace asked, smiling. "They'll come with glasses. Cardboard, you know. Retro and modern, all at once. Super cool, huh?"

Exactamundo. Mounds of molded plastic or rubber or something synthetic made it topographical. A three-dimensional T-shirt. Awesome.

She was in her element, this gal. The new product line was underway, and so was the publicity and outreach blitz. One guy was writing the blog, based on random thoughts that I had scratched down on bits of paper over the years.

Grace knew the real deal was social media. I had thousands of Facebook friends and followers. So many folks "liked" me and the photos that we posted. And my tweets were all the rage. They were ghost written too, but in the right spirit. Grace approved everything.

"No, Birch. Not wise," she had said, politely condemning my choice for a new name with enough sternness to make her point.

See, I had thought about rechristening myself as "The Rockin' Robin," what with all the tweets, but Grace said it didn't really make any sense, and that the phrase was probably copyrighted or trademarked, and we didn't need another *Death Wish* debacle. Smart cookie, this gal.

So we went with her idea, and it was a good one. It did the trick, and pretty quickly too. She worked the press for days and days about the reboot, and then came the launch.

The Artist 2.0: Shaping a Better Tomorrow, in Three-Dimensions.

All the products and tweets heralded the transformation. Instead of depicting me with my signature paintbrush or 9mm, publicity photos showed my hands working a mound of clay. I was the same, but I was different.

That was when I pitched my idea of using the handle "The Sculptor Formerly Known as The Artist," but Grace steered me away from that. Too long, she advised, and too similar to "The Artist Formerly Known as The Artist." No, the new name was already decided. It was The Artist 2.0. And you know, I agreed. In fact, the changes inspired me to repaint Frog, giving him an even bigger smile.

At first, a lot of people plain didn't know what to make of what was going on. Conservative politicos avoided me like the plague. The AM radio crowd jeered. And these days, even though Robert spent most of his time advising America to wise up about President Mullins, he got in a few zingers about the man he called "The Traitor Formerly Known as The Artist." No big deal, and besides, you couldn't really sue him over it anyway. I had asked just to be sure.

College Republicans dropped me flat too, but quite a few others in the 13 to 25 age range stood beside me. State and local politicians in Oklahoma and the states where I'd shot people, well, they adopted a wait-and-see approach. Their advisors told them to hold off, especially since they'd given me a free ride while I was the darling of WNB. No need to appear hypocritical until they had to, especially since some of them would be up for re-election soon.

Besides, pollsters claimed that thirty-two percent of Americans did not want The Artist arrested. And nineteen percent of them said that they would support me whatever I did. 'Course another ten or eleven percent didn't even know who I was. Fame has a ceiling. Always.

The amazing thing about my numbers was the fact that, even as my conservative base evaporated, millions of independents and more than a few liberals came to my side, or, more accurately, to the side of The Artist 2.0. Some of them even defended my brand of artwork as freedom of expression. They talked about the First Amendment and all that jazz.

Thanks to the filmmaker on staff, I not only had Facebook and blogs and tweets, but also a home studio where we could shoot exclusive content. Most of my own programs were thirty-seconds long. Kind of like political ads, but instead of selling candidates, they were selling ideas. Ideas and T-Shirts.

I also cut an album, which we called *Jump the Gun*. Now, truth be told, I can't sing, I can't play an instrument, and I'm rhythmically-challenged. That's what Grace said. Rhythmically-challenged. She was P.C., but hey, nobody's perfect.

To make the music work, I spoke my lines while some musicians played in the background. I wanted to get Asia to back me up, or at least some eighties dudes who knew how to rock, but Grace put down a veto. She wanted something trendy, something new. And so the result was kind of alternative-rock-reggae fusion. Ehh.

It was hard to find a good place to debut the album, since there aren't any more record stores. So the word went out on Facebook to flash mob at Venice Beach. Me and the band were there to sell LPs. Knowing that some of today's cool kids actually buy records, Grace let me win that fight.

Among other cuts, I performed the track *Common Sense Ain't Common No More*. Then, when all the vinyl sold out, I opened the trunk of my rental car and started giving away cassettes that I had copied and labeled myself. Grace hadn't known about *Birch's Mix Tape*.

But she did know that the buzz was great, and it gave her the courage to go All the Way. She hired more people, so many that I gave up on learning their names. But the nameless workers worked, and they worked hard and fast to get everything in place for our march on the National Mall.

It was warm that summer day in D.C., but it was also cool. Six straight hours of music and political talk. Several bands got everyone in the mood. Grace claimed some of them were in the Top Forty. I shrugged, but not because I didn't believe her.

Three politicians spoke, moderates all. One was a retired Republican; another a retired Democrat. The third was the Governor of Minnesota. She'd started her career doing voiceover for cartoons, but got into politics when that dried up. Running as an independent, she'd squeaked out a narrow victory a couple years back.

When I took the stage at the tail end of it, the cheers kept going for fifteen minutes. Well, maybe only two or three minutes, or even just thirty seconds, but it seemed like a lot longer. And there were thousands, or at least hundreds, of flashes going off, which made me bemoan the fact that no one uses flashcubes anymore.

Though I'd spoken to crowds so many times before, this was my biggest and most important gig, so my voice wavered a bit when I began. But by the time I got to the meat of the speech, I was in great form:

> *Common Sense. It's so uncommon, really, like the world's most precious commodity. I'd suggest some folks look it up in the dictionary, but maybe they still wouldn't understand it. But we've got to let the light in. I know that now.*

*Sometimes force is necessary. Sometimes we have
to fight. I have fought, time and again. Don't
tread on me, you know. But somewhere along
the way, maybe even from the very beginning, I
chose my battles unwisely. I've loved and lost. I
really have. But together, you know, we can pave
a new road.*

*Let's give the good people a chance. We'll fight.
Sure we will. But only when we have to. And
we'll do it the smart way.*

The crowd ate it up with a spoon, even though there
wasn't much to it. Touchy-feely and sappy. It didn't
matter, though, because they'd forget the words as soon
as they heard them. After all, I really speak through my
art. I always have.

Once the applause started to wind down, it was time
to wind it back up. And that was going to happen thanks
to the sculptor. He'd worked hard to bring Grace's con-
ception to life. No more canvases. The new piece was
full-on 3-D. And it was huge.

I yanked the cord, and the enormous sheet fell away,
laying bare the statue to the crowd and to the TV cameras and to all of America, at least that percentage who
knew who I was.

It was a stone version of me, wearing a Revolutionary
War uniform and beating on a drum. Over my shoulder
was a musket, ready to use, but the statue version of me
was playing music instead. Artistic and peaceful, but not
wussy. Definitely not wussy. I had become America's new
pet rock.

CHAPTER 34

Magic Trick

"We've re-branded, and we've been really effective with it," Grace said encouragingly.

"And?"

"And so let's just ride the wave, Birch."

She was right. She usually was. But some things take precedent over being right, or being correct, or even being smart.

"This is dumb," she told me. "This is a dumb idea, and I'm not going to let you do it."

"C'mon, I am dumb. I should have gone into some other line of work, you know, maybe a lawyer like Chet, and had a family and a picket fence."

"And a wife that tells you what to do?"

"You seem to be giving a lot of orders lately."

"They'll arrest you for sure if you go through with it."

"It'll be easy."

"How will you even get inside? They'll never let you near the place."

Maybe she was right, but I thought I had it all figured. Drive to Newark, hide the car at the airport, and get a cab into Manhattan. It'd probably cost eighty bucks, maybe one hundred with the tip and the toll, but this would be worth its weight in gold. And I would time everything based on when Robert was live.

As my cab approached WNB that afternoon, I fixated on the word "Firearm." Who came up with that word? They were really two words, "fire" and "arm," that someone jammed together. But why would you combine those words? Why create a new word using those two words? Was some poor idiot shooting a blunderbuss one day and it exploded, catching his arm on fire? Or did the guy who invented the word mean that the gun *was* an arm, like a third arm? Fire Arm. Firearm.

"Ninety-two fifty."

I could hardly make out what the guy said.

"Ninety-two fifty."

I still couldn't understand the guy's accent, but then saw the readout on the machine. Out came my wallet and five twenties. Before handing over the cash, I asked for a receipt. This was a business trip, so it was probably tax deductible.

The guy stared at me unhappily for a second after he took the hundred bucks, like he was expecting a bigger tip. Yeah, right.

The WNB reception area was nice, but sterile. It was a thin, narrow room, shotgun style. No pictures on the cream-colored walls. Short brown carpet, very industrial. A few plush seats and a sofa, all in brown. They were a different brown than the carpet, but not so different as to create the proper two-tone effect.

Two security guards stood near the front door. At the opposite side of the room, a long table went from wall-to-wall, kind of like the check-in desk at a hotel. WNB had never sprung for the obligatory fountain. That's conservatism for you. Saving money and unnecessary trips to go pee, all thanks to a single decision.

When I walked in, the security guards mumbled something to one another, but they didn't stop me. The receptionist stood. That or she was sitting on a tall stool. I couldn't figure how she got behind her countertop desk each morning, since it did extend from wall to wall. Maybe part of it lifted up, or maybe there was a secret passageway that led back there.

"Good morning, sir. How may I help you today?"

"Robert Lynch, please."

"He's in the middle of a live broadcast, sir. Is he expecting you?"

"No. I mean yes."

"I'm sorry?"

"The Artist 2.0."

"Oh, yes, yes of course. But I don't think he had any guests scheduled for today."

"Just here to say hi."

"Let me call up. I should check with…"

"Don't bother. I'd like to surprise him. Really."

I gave her the sweetest smile I could muster.

"Well…"

The receptionist hesitated. Then her face looked like she was scrolling back through every time Robert had been rude to her. She had a knowing look in her eye, but I didn't know what she knew. When she spoke, her face slowly transformed into a chuckle.

"Go on up. I'm sure he'll be happy to see an old friend."

And that was that.

I said virtually the same thing to the third floor receptionist, and it worked again. And then again to the guard at the studio door, except his eyes lit up and he asked if I was a famous TV preacher. Each time I was polite, and each time I got a polite response. I even blessed the guard. No problem. Go right ahead. Right in there, sir. These were good people, as polite as any ATM that I'd ever met.

Robert was already deep into his schtick. He had several props at hand, including a top hat, white gloves, and a cane. He was dancing down a staircase that only had about ten or fifteen steps, like he was in a Hollywood musical. It was all to illustrate some point or other, about how the President was doing a song-and-dance act to the American public.

Robert snapped the cane in half and threw it down. He took off the top hat and turned it upside like he was a magician.

"Wise Up, America! The President cannot pull a rabbit out of his hat. Not anymore. His day is done. His time is up."

After collapsing the top hat, Robert frisbeed it out of camera range. Then he walked over to his desk and sat down. His right hand clapsed his left. He shook his head up and down while his upper teeth softly bit down onto his lower lip. It made him appear sincere and gave him a few needed seconds to kick his shoes off under the table and secretly slide into a pair of slippers.

"Listen, America. I'm scared for you, and for my children, and especially for my children's children. We are on the wrong path. The President's high taxes have paid for the handbasket. A one-way ticket to Hell. That is, unless we can change things for the better. And, hey, I'm an optimist. All of you know that. We *can* change things. And we *will*."

He cleared his throat.

"The best solution is obvious. President Mullins should just off himself. He should just walk right out onto the White House lawn and kill himself, right in front of the White House press corps. And of course if they had any brains, since most of them are liberal too, they should follow suit and do the very same. It'd be like Jonestown, but this time with a purpose, and hey, I'd be okay with that. I mean, really. These folks have been drinking the crazy liberal Kool-Aid for years."

"Mullins," Robert said, rolling his eyes. "We can't count on him to be brave enough to do anything like that. Of course, our friend Pandro could take care of him real quick if he was being treated like the hero he is and not like some kind of criminal."

My mind drifted back to the JFK assassination, as it so often did. I remembered every frame of the footage from when Jack Ruby shot Oswald. Ruby seemed to shout the name "Oswald" right before firing, and so without thinking I did something similar. I was a good thirty feet away from Robert, but I shouted "Lynch," and then fired a bullet at Robert's belly. Ruby didn't miss; I did.

Robert's eyes flared, and his face went pale white. He said nothing, but he rabbited behind the rafters they used for the occasional live audience. I followed, but the cameras didn't. Nor did the camera operators, who just froze. I could swear one of them winked at me, but maybe my mind made that part up.

From the control booth, Tab ordered a commercial break. I couldn't hear him, but I caught a glimpse of his lips moving behind the glass. There wasn't much time.

Turning back towards me briefly, Robert looked like he wanted to shout, "Fuck you," but he couldn't. His mouth moved, but he couldn't say anything at all. Maybe he'd swallowed his own tongue.

Hot on the heels of my old pal, I ripped a Smith and Wesson .38 Special out of the shoulder holster. That was Grace's last request. If you have to shoot someone, don't use a 9mm again. You've been re-branded, so you can't look back. You can't go for the expected. And since Manhattan is not a Mannlicher-Carcano kind of town, I selected a wheel gun. It seemed more appropriate, a more mature way of handling things, because I didn't have anything against Robert except for his existence.

Banking a corner, Robert's right foot slipped out of his slipper, causing it to launch behind him like a pitiful torpedo. He trudged ahead, but to no real advantage. After another frantic gallop or two, his left foot slid out of his other slipper, thus bringing an end to his forward locomotion.

Somehow Robert's pudgy body wrenched in the process of falling, his face smashing into the rafters. His hands flew to his bloodied mouth. One or two of his front teeth had chipped.

I lifted the revolver, but Robert said nothing. Instead, he moved his hands from his mouth to the back-of-the-side-of-his-head, as if to protect it from imminent attack. Then he clenched his eyes shut. Maybe he thought that if he couldn't see me, then maybe I wasn't really there.

But I was there, rebooted to boot. And I wouldn't resort to the past. Instead, I did something else that Chet had suggested. I improvised. Without blinking or thinking, I fired two shots, one into each hemisphere of Robert's body.

Robert twitched a bit, so he probably wasn't dead yet. I knelt down beside him and said "Risome," but wasn't sure why. Then I shot him again. Magic things come in threes.

Tab kept the commercials going, because otherwise there would have been dead air.

CHAPTER 35

Beginnings

Washington, D.C. is a clean city. At least Capitol Hill is. The streets are spic-and-span. The Capitol Building looks spotless, like you could eat right off of the dome. It's white. It's really, really white.

I couldn't figure out what they did to keep it looking so clean, but they must do something. Sitting in a waiting room at the White House, I speculated as to whether they used high-powered hoses to wash it off, or if they just keep painting and repainting it, each new coat hiding the dirty old one.

It was an honor to be inside those hallowed halls, especially for somebody in my line of work. Pandro was in the lockup, but there I sat, about to meet the President. It had been in all the papers and on TV.

Of course, I had been told in advance that there wouldn't be a photographer present, but it was still a major score. Even the limo driver could see that.

"Good luck with it." Those were his parting words, voiced through a toothy grin. He wasn't so bad after all, I guess. My psychiatrist always reassures me that I'm a nice person, and so I need to be nicer to other people.

By that time, most politicians avoided me. The Majority Leader had tried to push through a resolution condemning my reboot, but there weren't enough senators willing to take a stand. A few folks in the House had praised my recent activity, but most congresspersons, well, they carefully steered clear of yours truly.

Once it got leaked that President Mullins would welcome The Artist 2.0, conservative talk radio went nuts. Some of them had mixed feelings when Robert got his just rewards. They agreed with him on most things, but that was the problem. He was their key competition. And he was on TV.

But for The Artist to visit the White House? Well, that was one step too damned far. Détente with the enemy, they cried. Belle Hewitt went so far to demand the abolishment of the National Endowment for the Arts. Of course, she had bleated on and on about the NEA many times before I ever arrived on the scene.

I no longer cared about such things, especially on the big day. I was more worried about talking to the President. *Mr.* President. Yes, that was definitely the best. My largest concern my *own* name. Do you correct the President if he calls you an assassin instead of a serial killer? And what if he addresses you as The Artist, instead of The Artist 2.0? 'Course if he says The Artist, it might be the result of brevity more than any intentional slight.

I had plenty of time to think. The President kept me waiting for two hours with no end in sight, all for a meeting that in the end had been downplayed. So much time had passed, or past, I thought while staring at my watch. Or, once I thought about it, when I *watched* my watch, which was itself watching something. Time, apparently. It was my timepiece. There's another funny word. It is a piece of time, but shouldn't it be timepieces, because isn't time plural, made up of all those seconds and minutes and hours?

That would probably cause a whole grammatical problem, though. Singular versus plural and all that. Like the word "people." Of the people and by the people. That's a singular word, or at least it doesn't have the letter *S* on the end of it, but it means more than one person. And more than one way of looking at the world.

"Excuse me, sir. We're ready for you now," the White House aide informed me. He was a big guy. Really big. He could have been a secretary or a strategist, but he was probably Secret Service. Maybe he was all three.

Deep breath, then release. My throat seemed to be swollen, or at least coated from the remains of my aging butterscotch.

"Right in here, sir," he instructed, opening the door to a big room with vaulted ceilings and a long table in it, like the type you'd use for important meetings.

Two other big Goons in suits stood at the back of the room. They were Secret Service for sure, because they were positioned right behind a sharply-dressed but very elderly man. He was already seated. Then the first guy pulled out a chair for me on the opposite end of the table. That precluded any handshakes, at least at the start of the meeting.

"Allow me to introduce the Vice-President," the first guy said after I sat down. He was referring to the old dude seated at the other side of the table.

This put an entirely different complexion on things. Nobody had ever said squat about the Vice-President. The lunatic fringe must have put the fear of God into the President, because I was getting the shaft. I knew it. And so did Frog, who was nestled safely inside my shirt pocket. Lordy. I should have upped my Prozac intake to 40 milograms a day.

"I understand you are a man out of time," the Vice-President said. His aged voice made him sound wise, but it was hard to tell if he really was.

"I'm sorry?"

"I read the article about you in *Esquire*. About how you aren't too keen on the modern world."

"Oh, that. Yes, sir."

"Then we are of the same mind, young man. I'm 86 years old. How about that?"

I forget which of the swing states the Veep helped put over for Mullins eight years earlier, but it was one of them. The years since had not been kind. He was too old and sick to run in the next election, so they'd probably put him out to pasture.

"You're a rascal, aren't you? I can see that from here," he said, smiling while he looked through his thick glasses.

"Yes, sir," I replied.

"What did you say? What did he say?" The Veep's hearing was on the blink.

"He said, 'Yes, sir.' " Evidently, the Goons were not mute.

"We hated to hear about your wife." The Veep projected a loud but frail voice, presumably so that I could hear him from so far away. Perhaps it was also a signal for me to speak louder.

"Well, thank you. Uhh, Mr. Vice-President, sir," I replied, turning up my volume.

"And please accept the President's apology for not being here today. Some urgent matters of state came up. In fact, I have to attend to them myself in just a couple of minutes."

"Yes. Yes of course. Mr. Vice-President."

His unsteady hand pulled a monogrammed handkerchief out of his coat pocket, which he used to wipe his nose. He didn't blow. He just wiped, and when he started speaking again, I saw a bit of leftover snot oozing down onto the wrinkles of his upper lip.

"Informally, off the record, you know, without ever being quoted, we think you have done your country a great service in recent days, particularly at the offices of WNB."

"Thank you. That's very kind. Uhh, Mr. Vice-President."

"And, also completely off the record, the President wants you to know that he understands that there are currently forces at work against you. There are those who want to see you behind bars. He has vowed, privately, off the record, to not let that happen."

During that last line, the Veep pointed to nowhere in particular, his weak forefinger so old that it was crooked. I didn't quite know how to respond, but by the time I said "Thank You" again, he had rasped out some more dialogue.

"Young man, the President will sign a full pardon for your acts of public service, but politically he cannot do that until the last day of his term."

"Yes. Yes, of course."

"Until then, I believe that you are seriously in danger of being indicted for Robert Lynch's murder. Seems like the FBI has collected some damning evidence."

His voice cracked when he spoke that last line, but I didn't know whether it was because of what he had just said, or because now he was even older than he was when our meeting began.

"Between you and me and the fencepost, Mr. Vice-President, I'm still not sure how I even got out of WNB that day. They had me, dead to rights."

The Veep wiped his nose again, then put the wet, squishy handkerchief back into his pocket.

"Our sources tell us that employees there waited a good while before calling the authorities. Seems like Mr. Lynch wasn't too popular with his colleagues. You've been one lucky guy, Mr. Barr, but your luck is about to run out. Soon. So I wish you well in trying to find some place safe for a few months."

"San Francisco?"

"That was where Pandro Burns got arrested, which suggests to me that they have a zero-tolerance policy for serial killers."

"Mexico?"

"If push came to shove, they would extradite you. And it's an easy place for bounty hunters to find you."

"Where then?"

"Ireland. Jerry Lee Lewis went there when he had tax trouble, and nobody messed with him. They're damned near a banana republic. Head to Ireland for an extended vacation, soon, before anyone hands down an indictment."

"Sounds like good advice."

"As part of this whole pardon thing, the President does hope that you'll be thinking seriously about what you are going to do now. And later." He pointed again with that crooked finger, but this time it seemed to be pointing my way.

"Huh?"

"It'll be easier for him to give you the pardon if you get into some other line of work, pronto. Announce your retirement from politics on the Google, or whatever the kids use now."

"But…"

"Son, my guess is that you've banked some money. Time to cash in the chips and leave the casino. A nice, discriminating young fellow like yourself…you should find someone to marry. Maybe have some kids. Time to settle down, Mr. Barr."

I didn't respond, but shook my head up and down a bit, as if to suggest I was seriously considering the idea.

"Settle down, Mr. Barr." He seemed aware that he was repeating himself.

After a few more seconds, the Vice-President looked over his shoulder and feebly waved his hand to signal the Goons. Each grabbed one of his elbows and helped him to his feet. His knees shook, so he held onto the table while a Goon grabbed his walker. At that point, the first guy began tugging at my own chair, a not-so-subtle prompt for me to stand up.

Then the Veep slowly ambled his way over to me, adding a few more steps to his life's extensive travels. No one said anything, so I focused on the sound of his movements, and on his nostrils, which forcefully inhaled a big wad of snot back down into his body. When he finally reached me, there was no handshake, but maybe that was because his hands clutched the walker like grim death. Anyhow, his voice had a softer, friendly sound to it, less formal than before.

"Young man, we need an answer on this, you know, now. If you want the pardon, that is."

His yellow eyes widened. There was still some life in the old boy yet.

"Is Pandro getting a pardon too?"

"Not a chance."

"Would it be okay to write a memoir?"

"An autobiography? Sure. But those need to be written in the past tense, you understand."

"I think so."

"So…what should I tell the President?" His eyes widened, waiting for my response.

What else could I do?

There was nothing else to do.

I chose, because I had no choice.